I0452824

FIRST LIGHT
AND OTHER STORIES

CATHERINE MINTZ

Published by Vivisphere Publishing 2000
Reissued by Copper Publishing 2017

www.copper-publishing.com

Cover art and interior art
copyright 2017 by Catherine Mintz

ISBN 978-0-9839589-3-2

TABLE OF CONTENTS

First Light

Lind froze in place, blinded by green afterimages. With her automatic glare filter turned off in the dimly lit bay, the security robot's red light dazzled her. The bot scanned her suit identification and accepted her voice command to switch off, move on.

The ship architect stayed still. There were too many wrong places to put her feet. *Holed by my own hull mine.* The surveillance system had caught a few crewmen sightseeing six or seven ship's-hours ago and Lind had sent in the bots.

Eyes closed, she listened to her suit puffing as it fought the cold. The *J-AO1, J-series Astronomical Observer One*, had started the plunge to near the cosmic background temperature. Twelve ship's-hours from now, its crew would board. The ship would be launched immediately thereafter, and renamed *Huygens*.

Already the *J-AO1* was in its natural element. The bay was separated from space only by grated safety gates. Except for the psychological comfort of being enclosed by *Los Angeles* and its frame of reference, Lind might as well have been floating in the open.

Vision restored, she blinked and looked about her. The huge construction bay was meticulously clean. The ship's builders had worked with gold and even more precious materials. Almost anything was harder to replace than recycle in the great deeps of space.

And, even if the shipwrights had been willing to waste anything, it would have been blown out with the residual air when the bay was decompressed. Some of that cloud of particles surrounding *Los Angeles* would go with the *J-AO1*. The craft's outer shell was a meter deep layer of ablative foam. Lind hoped it would be enough protection against the inevitable launch debris.

Now, beyond the grating, she could see stars. Lind inched forward. No human hand had touched the streamlined reflective white hull that stretched away into the dimness. Real or slaved robots had done most of the construction, and what human workers there were had been completely suited inspectors.

The one exception was the sealed living-control module that had only been joined to the main frame today. Inside that had the subtle irregularities produced by human hands, plus color, 3-Ds, music, soundscapes, and privacy soundproofing: six people would be spending a long, long time together.

Those remaining on *Los Angeles* could hope to return to Earth to live out their late middle age and senior years. The observatory ship riders were unlikely to meet humanity in the flesh again.

Some had left eggs, sperm, clones, or frozen children-to-be behind them. Others had not, fearing that they themselves would fit in only with their own kind and their children would be considered odd or pitiable. One or perhaps two had given offspring to their close kin or friends in discreet adoptions.

Lind had done none of these. Building ships she had designed was to be her life's work. She had thought it would be enough, but here, scanning for one last time the glassy hull that would be continuously robot-renewed throughout the *Huygens'* life—here, she was not so sure. *I designed it*, she thought, *but I—*

"Lind?" came the query in her ear. It was John Coltsfoot, second in command of the project and likely successor, should one be needed.

"Coltsfoot?"

"We're no longer losing heat from the bay. I think we're close to temperature turn-around. Unless you've found a problem, you might want to leave."

Diplomatic, she thought. *Had it been me on the intercom, I would have had a few things more to say.* "Thank you," she said. Coltsfoot would have waited until the last possible moment. It was the way he was. Safe behind her reflective faceplate, Lind grimaced. *Damn.*

An impenetrable façade was one of the burdens of command. Not for senior officers the cozy camaraderie of the mess. The Code said, "There must be a distance, graciously maintained, between those with rank and those without."

Glancing at the red time check at the corner of her faceplate, Lind lengthened her stride, felt the foot walk flex under her. *Ten hours and counting.*

Time was when maintaining command distance had been easy for her, but as the voyage grew longer Lind sometimes wished she were as free to remake herself as her project members. She missed the warmth of human contact.

But, she reminded herself, *if stone-faced posturing becomes unbearable, I can resign, become one of the crew*. Some other competent person would be elevated to her position. *Coltsfoot, probably*. He wanted the job, would not have been suitable if he were not ambitious.

Nothing is forever in the deeps of space, but Lind found the very thought of leaving her post to her excellent second, who apparently lacked the assertiveness that made a good boss— although he had no other flaw—repellent. She walked faster, eager to get inside.

Any project had to stop at some arbitrary degree of fulfillment, and this one had approached ideal more closely than most. Listening to her feet hit the plating, Lind was a long way from demoting herself.

It's stopping improving it that's hard. Imagining patting the hull in farewell, she looked instead. *It looks old.*

Designed for extended in-system work without a refitting dock to return to, *JOA-1* lacked the usual lumps and bumps of equipment despite multiple redundant systems packed within its sleek hull.

But the materials *JAO-1* was made of were unimaginable in the past. Six great braided-carbon struts, capped together at each end, and then wrapped tightly with filaments that were one long molecule made its frame. The spaceship's hull was a composite used by special permission of the military.

Its outer shell was foamed silicon, constantly under repair by its team of robots. During the launch the spidery hexagons would retreat to their lairs, ready to emerge if needed. From then on, under almost any conditions, they would be on patrol—not just to protect against disaster but also to insure a good return on a massive investment.

When carbon fibers and composite failed they did so catastrophically. The tension that held *JAO-1* together and rigid would tear the whole apart. Watching simulations, it was easy to envision helpless, suitless bodies tumbling as virtual atmosphere met virtual vacuum. Lind had deepened the ablative layer again and again. Foam was cheap, personnel and equipment expensive.

"Lind?" a quiet voice in her ear reminded her.

"Yes." She lingered a moment more, then said, "On my way."

When the request for proposals was posted, Lind had fought long and hard to justify what she submitted. Her design had looked *right*. Every line and curve served a purpose, formed a pleasing whole. After all these centuries, human eyes still hungered for the organic forms of the Great Home World.

Passing the midpoint on the way back, the architect checked her sleeve readout and sped up. *JAO-1* was a long ship: all three of its major elements needed to be separated from one another.

The instrument array traveled before the ship on an insulated spar, so the space it sampled and flew through was uncontaminated. The package shelter and repair pod was the first element of the spacecraft proper. The crew quarters were amidships so they could not leak heat to the array nor absorb particles from the drive. The main drive was at the rear and as far

from the other components as possible given the strength of
available materials.

Passing under the great wheel of the solar panels and approaching the boom that supported the maneuvering jets, Lind
paused. No matter her haste, she would spend a moment here,
where a shadowy twin of hers emblazoned the white hull.

She admired the pristine sweep, and then frowned. There,
on that spar, someone had lettered *JAO-1*. That touch of paint
would do no harm, probably. It was the principle of the thing
that had left the rest of the ship white, unmarred. She reached,
to hold her reader closer to the potential damage—

—her boot cling failed. One heel free, Lind froze, heart
hammering in her ears. She didn't want to leave her mark on
her creation by crushing its protective layer into a suit-shaped
hollow. The damage could be repaired quickly but the scar
would be visible during the launch.

Think your way out of it.

If she didn't solve this problem, someone would have to
come and haul her in. She could not use her propulsion pack: it
produced heat. Her quick-release safety line, so convenient,
looked unexpectedly frail. Lips pressed together, Lind pulled
on it slowly, slowly, drew herself to her knees, recycled her
suit functions. Setting her free heel down hard, she felt it take,
and sighed in relief.

I really am late.

Standing up, placing each foot precisely on the yellow center line, Lind hurried. The thrum of the plating underfoot tri-
umphant in her earphones, she reached the caged section seated
against the solid bulk of the mother ship, *Los Angeles*. She
latched the door grate, took one deep, relaxing breath, and then
another.

Safe. Comparatively safe.

She laid a gloved hand on the *Los Angeles*'s sturdy hull.
JOA-1 would have been a much frailer construct than it was if
Sam Ho had not invented a new type of drive, not as powerful

as those used on interstellar ships, but hotter and cleaner, a magnetically bottled yellow sun that released a miniscule jet of hot plasma.

That was a game-changer. Lind had modified her plans and the construction division had toiled long and hard, inventing whole new techniques to bring the revised vision to reality—

"Countdown begins. Take your posts," said her helmet earphones.

—the all-channels communications feed had began. Overhead, warning lights blinked on. The launch remained on schedule, even though Lind was later than she'd planned. The ship architect was only at the outermost airlock and should be on board.

Given how gifted a designer Ho was, Lind had been surprised when he had added his name to the roster of people requesting they be considered to crew *Huygens*. He was a social kind of person. A six-person astronomical observer seemed an unlikely choice for him to make for the rest of his life.

Inventing her own protocol, Lind had called Ho in. It was a forlorn hope that there be something that would change his mind but she had to ask. For the record, if nothing else. "Why do you want to go?" Lind said bluntly, conscious of the omnipresent recorder.

"Hard to explain," he replied.

"Perhaps it's not a good idea," she suggested. "Or maybe there's something we need to give you here, more assistants, more autonomy?"

He shook his head, almost absently.

Then, taking a deep silent breath, Lind said, "You know how important a member of the team you are. The end of a project is always disheartening."

He shook his head again. "No. I have to think how to tell you without wasting your time." Ho paused, looked up. "Let me tell you a story, with the understanding that I could give you references, dates, names and so forth."

"All right," said Lind.

"Traditionally, before much was known about materials, before there really was science, building was an art." Having begun, Sam settled back in his seat, relaxed. "For generations, my clan did this kind of work. We assembled every scrap of knowledge we could on how to build stronger, taller, deeper, lighter. Whatever might be necessary for some new task—"

His big, strong right hand gripped an imaginary handle.

"—an apprentice would learn from her master how to do something that worked, and she, in turn, would show her apprentices, and so on. Every once in a while, someone would innovate, and occasionally they had a success. Success or failure, we would see what there was to be learned—"

Lind settled back herself. She had taken a course in the history of her profession, but it had not covered the great chain of people that had carried craft knowledge through the ages and times when there were no databanks, libraries, or even widespread literacy.

"—now. Consider the bridge builders," continued Ho, "working without Virsak—

The ship's architect, whose *JAO-1* had at first been a huge version of a bridging span spar, the kind that was the basic structure of almost every station, leaned forward. She had spent months assembling data and weeks more building a virtual simulacrum. Building it any other way seemed impossible.

She had never considered what one would do without such equipment. Her gut twisted a trifle: so many things could go wrong. Testing in miniature had its limits, even if you compensated by using frailer materials. Just the strength of a cross-braced joint could give a false result. She remembered a class when she'd—

The ship architect came back to the here and now with a slight jerk.

If Ho noticed, he gave no sign of it.

"—done. The master then staged a ceremony. He, his workers, and carts filled with enormous loads, would move onto and across the bridge to prove with their very lives that it could bear more much more weight than it would ever need to in normal use."

"Ah," said Lind, seeing the point. "And you want to 'test the bridge.'"

Ho nodded. "I do."

"You don't have any doubts?" Ho might prefer death to the disgrace of failure, particularly if anyone died because he had not gotten everything right—or right enough. "Because if you do, I need to know them now. Maybe it's ethical for you to risk your own life, but I can't risk others unnecessarily. Not to mention the materials and effort." *And the five more ships I hope to build.*

"No," he said. "None. I may never do anything more important, and I want to go with the *Huygens*. And I *am* the most qualified person to report how the ship handles."

Lind waited but Ho said nothing more. He didn't need to. Policy on these matters had been debated hard and long in other times and other places. The decision was *hers*. The ship builder could just follow precedent; retain Ho because he was useful.

Ho was not given to impulsive decisions. Lind was, sometimes. Her father had teased her about her "feminine instincts" until she concealed the trait, but it had not gone away. "You're on the roster," she said. "I'll miss you. No one else could have built that drive."

"Well," he said, "you have the drive, my reports and extrapolations for the ships to come. There shouldn't be any difficult problems, just fine-tuning. I'll send new data when there's any opportunity. I think—"

"You're rostered," Lind said, cutting him off.

He would do his best. They would do their best without him being with them. She was very tired and there was a long day to come. They would all be long ones until the *Huygens* was on its way.

"Yes ma'am." Ho had left without another word.

Back in the present, Lind blinked, and blinked again, her shadow coming and going as the warning lights blinked. She was bone-tired, living on adrenalin. After the launch she and her team could party, sleep, and think of something other than shipbuilding for a while.

She supposed she looked forward to that.

JAO-1 would be the only ship in this solar system. Veiled by gas clouds, with one deep green planet, which did not display the complete spectrum of chlorophyll and yet suggested it, this might even be the place where they would find life as fully developed as Earth but entirely different.

Or it might be just another ecological system of non-sentient mutations of the hypothetical star seeds that had brought life everywhere humans had found it. Everywhere people had been, living things shared the same basic patterns. It had long since separated into different strains, but the tree-like pattern of relationships was there.

Religion proclaimed all life was one and this proved the existence of God. The ship architect remembered one televangelist shouting, "We look upon his very face and yet some deny it!" A simple worldview. Hers was more complex. For one thing, why had they found nothing sentient—

"Now hear this. Launch safety protocols have been initiated for sectors A, C, G, and—"

Time to go in. Lind dropped her earphone sound level to the minimum, looked around. Tomorrow this foot walk would be pulled away. Then the only access to *JAO-1* would be through the flexible hose airlock mated with the *Los Angeles*.

More warning lights came on, casting multiple shadows. Fusion drive ignited. Now it was building toward thrusting power. It would not be more than hypothetically dangerous for some hours, yet Lind shivered, just a little. *Time to go in. One last thing to do*.

Unlocking and lifting a cover, she toggled the switch that drew the walk in and command-locked it down early. That would isolate the heat she had introduced. It would also keep other sightseers away.

Stepping through the double valves, Lind closed them solidly behind her, locked them, too. They would not be opened for anything but routine checks to keep them from vacuum welding until the shipwrights began constructing the next ship, the *JOA-2*. There were improvements she intended to make—

Unsuited, Lind opened one door and then another, was, finally, where she was supposed to be on the timeline, in the shipwright's section on her way to command. "Coltsfoot? On board, in section."

"Ma'am."

Shipwright space was almost riotous. The prevailing hair color had become a fiery orange and standard issue body suits had been slashed to reveal a great deal of bare skin, some of it better left covered. Everyone not involved in the launch was high on excitement.

Lind directed that the non-working crowd move back, told someone to activate a stand-back line on the floor. The launch techs were at their posts, eyes on boards and displays that were counting the moments and completed sequences, everything on schedule, ready.

The *JAO-1*'s crew was easy to pick out of the happy crowd. Man and woman they wore plain, as-issued liners, prepared to enter their hard suits for the release and the first full-scale firing of the new engine. Sam Ho looked confident; the rest looked like they had not eaten much recently.

The six were drawing together, all the good-byes they wanted to say said, all the cheeks kissed, all the final embraces truly final. If Lind could have advanced the timetable for their sake she would have, but every test must be run, run again, and then run for a third and last time.

"Coltsfoot," Lind yelled, and he came weaving through the crowd, having somehow managed to be one with the gaudy revelers and yet retain his dignity of rank. Admiring his ease, she made a mental note to think about how to better handle such things herself. *Just not right now.*

"Ma'am," he said.

"Clear everybody who's not working back into the recreation area. Take it slow but I want them out of here in fifteen minutes. Get them to want to go. Turn on the music, set the snacks out, get all screens imaging."

"Ma'am," he said again and was gone. There were whole days when he said nothing else. His lack of small talk or frank advice got annoying sometimes, but not now.

Lind flinched as the audio system came on, too loud, and then faded into leakage from behind the rec area doors. In Brownian motion the crowd began to flow toward the sound of Party.

None too soon, either, for as soon as the cheerful riot was hidden if not inaudible, the double doors through to *Los Angeles*' main decks opened. This was an event in itself. The galactic starship was military, and its crew of thirty-year recruits was rigidly segregated from the civilians, the shipwrights.

Given that both groups would spend most of their lives inside the same hull, one might have expected at least some formal mingling. There was an enormous need to enliven long periods of tedium separated by a month or two of desperate endeavor and a few moments of sheer terror.

But Captain Nguyen had elected not to use the power of discretion Lind knew she had. *Los Angeles* was run strictly according to regulations, even though it had been detached for a mission neither military nor political. The ship architect would have appreciated a looser approach. Suppressing a sigh, Lind went to greet the Captain with proper enthusiasm.

Nguyen, faultlessly attired, groomed, and coifed—rumor had it there were two crew people who were assigned to keep her looking just so—looked around with an air of restrained disapproval. Impaled by that cold stare, Lind spoke. "A pleasure to see you, Ma'am. Things are well in hand."

"What's that noise," said the Captain. It was not a question but a contradiction and a demand for an explanation in one.

"Some of the off-shift crew are being a bit premature," said Coltsfoot, unexpectedly right at Lind's elbow. "Ma'am decided to move them out of the way and not waste time."

The ship architect reminded herself, once again, to appreciate her second.

He continued, "It's been a long project and success has overwhelmed them."

"By the Code, I've little power to control their leisure," added Lind, who had seen this as a potential source of trouble when she accepted the position—and still did. There were many things one could do in one's off-duty time, not all of them leading to clearheaded team members.

Nguyen had resisted increasing Lind's authority.

The Captain glared at the rec area doors, which seemed to pulse slightly to a pseudo-sense beat. "*I* have the authority," she said, and gave Lind an icy glance.

The ship architect felt a year had been taken off her life. "It might be wise to restrain them," said Lind, as if taking advice. She had already put anyone she might possibly need on standby, but a wise subordinate is agreeable to a superior, even if the superior isn't precisely in the line of C and C.

"Indeed," said Coltsfoot. "In case of an emergency, there is no predicting who might needed or useful."

"Do you want to make that a formal request," the Captain asked Lind, knowing that the architect did not. There wasn't the slightest inflection of a question.

"No, Ma'am," she said. "We're a small group." There were people all around, although none of them were obviously listening and most were clearly focused on the job at hand. Nguyen would know the problems of maintaining a working relationship with so small a number of people. You did not pull rank unnecessarily. You did not *interfere* unnecessarily.

Now the recreation area doors were shuddering from the beat for a mirror line. Nguyen looked at the vibrating panels with a chilly smile then, at Lind and grinned.

It was ghastly.

"I think I'll just look in on the party. All right with you?"

The ship's architect nodded, yes, and exchanged stares with her wide-eyed second. That visit was going to cool things down fast. Nguyen was no fool.

The rec area doors opened before the Captain, and, although she was not announced, as she would have been in her own areas of the ship, the clamor died in less than fifteen seconds.

"Carry on," commanded Nguyen, and there came the noise of people pretending to have a good time, until the doors closed.

Lind looked at Coltsfoot; then they both lost the fight and grinned.

"It is a better working environment," said Lind, surveying all the silently eloquent backs bent before projectors and touch consoles.

"Ma'am," choked out Coltsfoot, with his face almost straight.

Even through the soundproofing, they could hear one of the Captain's escorts bellowing for punch for the Captain. Lind hoped he used a sniffer before he handed it to her. Some of the construction crew had boarded with nothing but pharmaceuticals for personal luggage.

Do your own job. She'll do hers.

Lind turned to watch the numbers run up the boards. The expected digits dropped into place. Without additional commands, her team began the main launch sequence. One by one,

21

the crew boarded through the flex hose lock and it was retracted.

Tick by tick, *JAO-1* lost the last of its residual heat, kept from collision with its mother ship only because the pair was moving at the same speed and direction, plus the restraint of a heavily-insulated safety whip.

Built to withstand the end-to-end stresses of the engine firing at the temperature of a hot sun while keeping the camera cold, once its power plant was on the *JAO-1* could be warped by heat leaked from the *Los Angeles*. From Nguyen's point of view, the ignited *JAO-1* was a bomb against the belly of her ship.

So there was deliberate haste to separate the two. False color displays let the observers see how the colored pattern of heat was shrinking. When there was nothing but rapidly fading pale marks where the cradles of the supporting arm had been, Lind said quietly, "Drop the whip," then, "*Jay-O One*, are you ready?"

It was the first time the ship's serial number had been used in ship-to-ship communication. "*Jay-O One*," responded the *J-series Astronomical Observer*. "May we be designated *Huygens*?"

"So noted," said Lind. "*Huygens*, we will begin primary launch sequence—now. Communications contact must be maintained until formally broken from this ship, *FTK42*, named *Los Angeles*."

"Acknowledged."

They sound crisp, thought Lind with pride. The *Los Angeles*' crew would have no reason to make fun of these civilians. A blast of solange beat shook soundproofed doors before it was turned down. *Well, not much reason*. Again she repressed awful suspicions about what might be in the punch.

The observation package was turned on. Looking at the screen for the optical camera, the ship architect saw nothing but her reflection against darkness. Then, so sharp and perfect that Lind didn't need the readouts, the disk of light appeared. "First light," she said softly through the communications system.

All around her she could hear the exclamations that told her that good data was pouring in through all the sensors. The image blurred. Her heart stuttered before she realized it was tears in her eyes and not some horrible fault in the lens. There was something poetic in the idea of light from so far away being blurred by human emotion, but Lind was not the one to make something of it.

She stood, her reflection overlying the field of stars, until it was crisp and filled with fine detail. Looking, her joy was so fierce it was like anger, shaking her whole body.

"*Huygens* to *Los Angeles*," said astronomical observer control. Lind leaned in to check the data feed. There should be no reason to speak. Machines were exchanging all the necessary information. Human communication was unnecessary, unwanted. At this critical moment words were far too slow.

"*Los Angeles*," replied the mother ship, since Lind has not spoken.

"We have a personnel problem."

Lind donned her command expression before turning around. If there were a problem, it would probably require *Los Angeles* act. The ship architect had limited powers when it came to using the larger ship's equipment and organization.

"Explain," demanded *Los Angeles* communications, then, without missing a beat, "Captain to the bridge!"

Someone switched the channel into open mode. Recognizing the terrified voice, Lind frowned. Jade Goldsmith, Sam Ho's partner, but not yet wife. Lind assumed Sam and Jade had been paired off by their elders, and were waiting some traditional period of time to be joined.

"Noo," wailed the young woman. "No! No!"

Goldsmith had signed Ho's petition-for-posting and had been added to the crew as if they were husband and wife. She was a passive personality, foil to the outgoing Ho, a reasonably good fit for the crew.

Lind had not liked the pair's decision not to make it permanent before they embarked. It wasn't as if there were going to be other eligible people around. Single, the two of them might destabilize social relations. *Why now*? she thought. *Should I have had them truth tested*?

The Captain was not going to be sympathetic.

Assuming Nguyen was still in a state to act.

The *Los Angeles* carried a dozen or more specialists to do interrogations. Lind would have had to request their services, get a waver of rights from each potential crew member, and Nguyen's formal, on the record, approval.

The architect knew some of her people would not pass the state religion section of the test. Born skeptics, they would die skeptics. In the positions they held, it did not matter, but they were not suitable for officers, and truth testing screened for the fleet, not for astronomers.

Nonetheless, Goldsmith's shrill shouts ringing in her ears, Lind decided from now on she was going to require truth testing for every about-to-be crew member. It was an insult to a dedicated group of people, but the project could not afford this mistake twice.

As for the immediate problem, it was late, but not too late to rectify the error. They would have to send the *Los Angeles'* skiff, which would be one big favor owed, payable sometime in the inconvenient future. Lind sighed. She hated *owing*.

"I don't want to go! Let me go back! I don't—" wailed through the *Los Angeles* followed by a mutter of other distant voices. Obviously Jade's fellow crew members were not dealing with things well. *Maybe on purpose*, thought Lind. Had she been on the *Huygens* she would have wanted this woman off, now. This was the last possible moment.

The *Huygens* officer finally keyed down the volume—Jade had begun a keening, wordless scream—and requested a local-limited mike kludge from his *Los Angeles'* alter ego, which would cut the transmitted sound to anything close to and in front of the console.

Her own communications officer looked to Lind. "Ma'am?"

"Ask what's going on," she said.

"Ah, *Jay-O 1*, this is project communications. Could we have a situation report?"

There was the sound of something crashing into something else. Then there was an enormous amount of yelling, followed by a solid thud.

"*Jay-O 1?*"

There was heavy panting and a new voice. "We need help. The ship's fine, but we need help. She's completely out of control. We've confined her to the core shelter." It was the sturdiest place on the ship and the only part designed to withstand any battering. Weight had always been a serious consideration in the *Huygens'* design.

"Confirmed, you need help." Communications turned to Lind.

"Help is on its way," she said immediately, and heard it repeated. Pulling an all-ship mike to her, she keyed it open and ordered, "Crisis team to the skiff!"

It was one of the few all-ship commands she could give without first consulting the *Los Angeles'* captain. It was gratifying to hear the distant rumble of opening doors and the wail of alarms that said she had been responded to without delay.

"We have a no-go from one of the crew," said the voice from *Huygens*. This was the formal announcement the records required.

"Copy, no-go from crew member. Stand by." Lind said, "We'll take her off."

"Ma'am?" The crews had been picked with care and there were no pre-selected backups. Her project communications officer knew that.

"You heard me. We'll take the woman off."

"*Jay-O 1*, Director Lind has directed the no-go be re-moved." The hideous sound of unreasoning terror stopped. Perhaps Jade was not quite so scared as she'd been acting. The ship architect doubted the news had been enough, but who could tell? Maybe they'd goosed her with a tranquilizer. Or three.

No ship was safe with someone out of control on board. It was legal and acceptable to kill them rather than attempt to re-strain them for any length of time. If Jade had cracked an hour or so later, then sedation and the ministrations of the auto doc-tor would have been the only other options to her execution.

Jade might have calmed down once going was inevitable.

But *might* was not acceptable.

As it was, they were beginning to edge into the *Los Angeles'* own launch window. The plans could be revised, if necessary, although half of her crew had already been packed down in long sleep. Pulling them out imperiled their health; leaving them in longer did the same.

Captain Nguyen was not going to be pleased.

What could they need that's not on board, Lind thought. The opportunity should not be wasted, even if all she sent was fresh fruit from the conservatory. "Get details," she told the of-ficer, "for the record, and tell them again help is on the way."

But, Lind reflected, *if I can, post-facto, spin the exercise in my report as a test of the recovery options for all the ships—*

That might go down well in the long run. In the short run, relations would be strained. *Which could be a good thing*, thought Lind. Her crew would be more alert to personnel prob-lems from here on out. Problems, but ones she could solve, even turn to good account.

Staring out at the glowing dot of the fusion drive that was all one could see of the *Huygens* at this distance, Lind felt a paradigm shift shiver through her. *I want to be on that ship. See what's on that planet. They need another crew member. I could go.*

26

One ear on the sounds of the skiff being loaded and crewed, minutes to make a decision about the rest of her life, hands shaking, Lind pulled up the charts. Scrutinizing Sam Ho's record was logical. It was the next step that came almost too close to committing her.

She asked for a compatibility check. Machine analysis, necessarily cruder than the slower method that included human observation plus testing over time, showed an eighty-five percent compatibility Ho-Lind. *I could manage it*, she thought. *It wouldn't even have to last. I can live single.*

In Lind's home, the undersea colony Tethys-BAO-7, marriages were made by the Directors based on genetic analysis. A progression of rituals committed the newly joined, stage by monitored stage. The isolation and danger on the drowned worlds were powerful binders. Few couples failed to complete the sequence.

As for the tight quarters on the ship, undersea colonies were confined environments. *I'm comfortable here*, she thought. Huygens *might be even better*. A whole dangerous solar system to explore with someone certainly trustworthy and at least agreeable. With that thought, Lind's decision was made.

"Coltsfoot!" she called.

"Ma'am."

"Congratulations on your promotion. I will be taking the place of the no-go, Jade Goldsmith, CS." She was sorry she would take no recording of Coltsfoot's expression with her, but then she was unlikely to ever forget it.

"Uh," he said, all his not-quite-plotting and careful planning gone to waste. He was faced with, *Here, you take it*, as she walked off from his idea of the ultimate plum of a job.

"Project Director?" It was thrilling to watch Coltsfoot realize he was the one the Captain was addressing.

"Sir?" he said, voice too high.

Lind didn't smile.

"Who's that?"

"Coltsfoot, sir."

"Where is Lind?"

"Sir, Lind has appointed herself to the crew of *Huygens* and appointed me to her position. She is, at this moment entering her formal statements. Sir. Ma'am."

There was a long silence during which nobody near a mike anywhere in the communications system said or did anything. That was something to be savored, too, although Lind was more than busy donning her suit.

She reviewed what she was leaving in her cabin. Since she'd always traveled light, and never been so foolish as to keep a personal log, there was nothing she needed retrieved.

"Ready, Sir," she said. Three people swarmed around her in verification, twisting seals, checking tension, tapping her tank for the sound it was full. It was an old drill, intended to be effective even without instruments to hand. It was also a traditional goodbye.

"Ready," said one, stepping back.

"Ready," said the second.

"All correct, Sir," confirmed the third.

"I'll miss you," said Coltsfoot, obviously puzzled by the emotion. It had not yet hit him that he would have five ships to build.

"Best of luck," she told him. "My notes are in my cabin if you need them."

"Thank you," he said, mechanically.

Then there was nothing more to do. Lind settled onto the passenger bench of the skiff, pushed the protective restraints on. A jumble of containers was loaded, tied in a net: messy but effective, and much, much faster than stowing.

The engines whined to life. Lind was pressed into her seat so hard she had a moment's difficulty breathing. The *Huygens* grew before her eyes, even as the background chatter told her Jade was ready to be removed, sedated, as a medical emergency.

Not my problem. I didn't know how tired I was of responsibility for so many people, so many things. This is *the right move.* Then, below and to their right, was *her ship*, white and new, its drive glowing on standby: picture-perfect. It became nothing but a wall, a lock, and then a blanked and shuttered port.

"Passenger to transfer," came the call.

"Transferring now."

Lind rose and glided through the air, braking herself easily with one hand. She swung into the lock, felt it thrum as it cycled her through, and was back in gravity, on the main deck, just behind the command bridge.

She released herself from her suit. There should be help here, but given the circumstances, its absence was excusable. Lind made no haste in getting out of her things: she was going to be here a long time, and there were no custom-fitted replacements ready on the *JAO*.

"Welcome aboard," said Sam Ho as he came through the door, face flushed with haste.

"It's good to see you, Sam," she said. "I thought I'd better test the bridge."

Ho grinned. "A fine old tradition," he replied and he took her hands in his.

Rachael Lind grinned back. *Bet he makes it formal*, she thought. *Not a competitor in a million miles and I still bet he makes it formal.* "I'm glad to be here," she said, their strong hands linked.

Then the signal sounded and they both headed for their stations: his at the engine console in the rear of the crew module; hers far down the hull where the readings from the instrument package's signals would be relayed.

THE WOMAN
WHO KNEW BETTER

Marilee banged the side of the old stove's firebox with a stick of kindling to break up the ashes, then shook the grate back and forth until the uncovered bed of coals glowed red and even. She held a hand in the oven as her lips moved in silent counting, then whipped it out, and slammed the door to, hand muffled by the edge of her apron.

It'd be just about right by the time she needed it.

She reached up to the second dresser shelf, and took down the biggest mixing bowl, the one that looked as if its rim had been dipped in thick buttermilk that had run, here and there, onto its sky blue belly.

Old Elijah Krober that was Dulcy's father—a good potter with a bad tongue in his head—had made it more than thirty years ago, before his kiln had burned to the ground and he and all his family had been killed. But the bowl was just as good as the day it was made. Better, maybe, for all its years of knowing batters and biscuits.

Marilee filled the sifter from the flour bin and brought it to the table, one hand under to save the floor. She shook four heaping handfuls into the bowl, then paused to tuck a loose strand of hair back into her tight, gray bun.

Then she was out the open door, across the well-swept yard, down among the pine trees of Dulcy's grove, going to the spring. There the butter crock sat nestled in the pebbled bottom, half hidden by the ripples. For convenience's sake the stoneware jar was secured by a string looped on an iron peg driven deep in the kneeling stone. Marilee knelt and pulled it out, automatically testing the waterlogged cord with a jerk between both hands. Still sound.

One hand on cold pottery, she stayed a moment to look at the pattern of branches across the sky, to listen to the sound of water spilling over into the patch of ferns downhill. Then her old knees protested the rock's smooth hardness just as her young ones had, and she rose quickly to her feet. Marilee had been kneeling there at least twice a day for sixty years and more.

She unfastened the crock from the string, made a tidy coil, knelt again to hang it on the peg, dipped her forefinger and drew a curlicue on the dry stone. Protection. Her great grandmother had done the same. Maybe her twice great gran, too. Slocum's was an old farm, with a date carved knuckle-deep in its thick, rough mantle. When they'd got the money for clapboards and the cabin was pulled down, the ancient chimney was left standing, and the new house built around it. The old place's well-seasoned logs had filled the fireplace the next winter.

But Dulcy's pool had been in use long before any log cabin had been here. There were arrowheads among the stones on the bottom, little ones, not much bigger than Marilee's thumbnail, black and thin, fluted along the edges where some ancient hand had knapped them. And before the worked stones had fallen in there had always been pebbles dancing in the boil, their fortune-telling patterns ignored by whatever came to drink.

Marilee looked and sniffed the air as she crossed the yard toward the weathered clapboard with its whitewashed door. Cold weather was nearly here. Having been battered by two seasons' worth of weather, the trees that climbed the hillsides all around had gone dull olive and rusty brown.

Brighter than gold, the late sunlight gilded each leaf of the maple at the gate. Its ragged crown shivered all over, once, despite the quiet air, then went completely still under Marilee's critical eye.

She frowned.

Slipping out from among the maple leaves were scraps of

white, furling and unfurling, which might have been errant but-
terflies from the cabbage patch, if Marilee had planted cab-
bages this year. They drifted toward the ground, blew across
the yard to linger above the doors of the old root cellar, then
slipped around the corner of the house and were gone.

Marilee sniffed again, quite differently. Uppity, they were.

Inside, she put the crock on the corner of the table and un-
tied the loop that held the wooden lid down. Cool water pooled
on the tabletop, was sopped up with a fast swipe of the oldest
dishtowel. She scooped out a lump of butter, half the size of
her fist, with a deft twist. It was almost the last—she'd have to
walk to Lester's tomorrow and hope his cow was still in milk.
Then the old pastry cutter thumped its way across the bowl and
back, fast as the hand could move, a blur to any watching eye.

It'd be biscuits, not cornbread, tonight. Fried ham. Greens
that had been slowly simmering all the long afternoon. The to-
mato preserves Mrs. Willis had brought in trade. Haw jelly.

Marilee took pride in setting a good table.

She rolled the biscuits out, cut them with a floured water
glass, lifted them onto the black baking sheet with a spatula,
moving faster now, with an eye on the sky out the window that
had somehow changed from afternoon to evening when she
wasn't looking.

Down to the spring with crock and bucket, back with the
bucketful of water for the first washing up, scrubbing the table,
rinsing the bowl, setting the iron kettle on the back of the
stovetop to heat for the real washing, after.

Quick, with a flick of her wrists, she shook the red-checked
tablecloth open in the air and settled it in place. Then the
wooden fork and spoon. The wooden-handled knife. The water
glass with a stenciled white and green design of orange blossoms. The napkin in its deal ring of four hands clasped together, the last of the set her old uncle had carved for herself
and her three sisters.

Marilee surveyed it all and pursed her lips with satisfaction.

A rainbird fluttered, frantic, against the lower panes of the window, and she took off her apron, leaned through the open door to shoo it away. She squinted up at the darkening sky. The lavender clouds were big-bellied with threats. Showers later, she thought.

Above the maple a cloudlet making its way against the wind caught her eye and stopped, drifting off unconcernedly, almost invisible against its bigger brothers billowing high in the air, their immense heights stained peach and rose with sunset.

Marilee sniffed once more, folding her apron crosswise then longwise into a tight, smooth bundle and draping it over one shoulder. Uppity. But it was about time anyway—dark *was* coming on. Already the tree shadows stretched long arms across the yard and the sun was down behind the hills.

She went over to the wooden, slanting doors of the old root cellar, drew the oak peg from the rusty hasp, and used it to rap on the planks. "Sonnyboy? You can come out now. Your things have been looking for you." She swung the hasp back on one side and stuck the peg back into the staple on the other.

One panel rose slowly up, releasing the scent of fresh-turned earth and rotting leaves. Something darker than the cellar's darkness growled and scrabbled at the iron door fastenings.

Marilee pulled the apron off her shoulder and fanned herself with the folded bundle. "Mind, don't hurt yourself. Sometimes I wonder if you have good sense." She looked into the gloom. "Come on up, now. Supper's ready."

There was a great whuff of dank air, and Sonnyboy's shaggy head peered out from the safe darkness. He mewed at the fading purple of the clouds.

"It's *past* sunset," said Marilee firmly. "Showers or no, your father'll be waiting by Crowther's farm at full dark."

Sonnyboy slobbered a little, and mounted another stair.

Marilee fanned herself a bit more and went on, "You'd think Japhet Crowther would have learned by now. I've lost count how many cows he's had pulled down." She eyed the massive, hesitating form. "He bought new hens last Tuesday. Tell your daddy to look for eggs—no use your trying to gather them."

The huge, taloned hands worked helplessly.

"Shame on you for being shamed," she said tartly. "You know how your father depends on you."

Wooden planks thudded, and dust pattered down. Sonnyboy rose out of the earth, step by step.

"It'll be nice after midnight," Marilee said, turning away to give him a moment's privacy while his eyes adapted. His eyes did tear so when he looked into the light. "This breeze'll blow the clouds right through."

Sonnyboy huffed, and smelled the rising wind. In the dusk he was an enormous blackness pestered by a swirl of tiny glowworms hard to make out even in the shadows beneath the trees.

Half-formed intentions, no doubt. Marilee knew better than to pay any mind. His daddy'd find work for his idle hands.

Thinking of Sonnyboy's father, she bowed her head in silent homage. Japhet Crowther was foolish not to pay his respects. Everyone hereabouts did, just like their families always had. It did no harm to be respectful.

The Old Powers could surely be touchy if you weren't. Only a fool would set himself up to go against them. Elijah Krober had been just such a one. Dulcy'd been the only one to escape when the kiln went.

Marilee remembered the girl, barefoot in her white night shift, standing right there under the maple, face dyed red by the light of a fire a good half-mile away. "He didn't mean it," she kept wailing. "He didn't!"

Hysterical, the sheriff from Bixby said, and the locals had muttered something like agreement. Someone hunted up an old blanket for the girl and someone else brought sweet tea in a cracked cup. The three county officers stood about, swag bellies hanging over their belts, fussing over Dulcy until the fire burned low. It was a drought year, and they'd only come to see

that the hillside didn't go, and a wildfire start on its way toward
Bixby.

The wind just eddied around and around in Krober's hollow,
building a pillar of flame that you could see for miles. The
blaze died before dawn, leaving nothing but the burned-out
kiln, the fireplace, and a few scorched trees.

A miracle, the sheriff said, in this dry weather.

Yes, indeed, everyone murmured. And it *was*.

Sonnyboy shuffled his feet and lifted his head to the growing dark. The first star winked on, then a second. Marilee's
mouth went prim. The Powers were mostly forbearing if a man
was drunk, sick, scared, or ignorant. But Elijah—

None of them had been surprised when the girl was found in
Slocum farm pool, her long hair floating like waterweed. "Seen
too much," said some of the old folks. "Made her bargain,"
other withered voices said. Marilee sniffed. As if *they* knew
anything. Dulcy'd read the patterns in the stones at the bottom
of the spring.

They'd buried the girl right *there*, under the pines—the
blanket, the cup, and the body in the same old shift she'd died
in. Death was a high price for a young girl to pay for her
daddy's mouth, but Elijah'd known better than to say what he
had. Respect was all the Powers demanded.

A course, if you offered more—

They could be neighborly.

Marilee suddenly smiled into the darkness. Fresh eggs
would taste mighty good, fried, with plenty of bacon. Sonnyboy liked bacon almost as much as he liked ham. Better, some
days.

"Supper," she said briskly, and went ahead to slake the
stove with ashes.

"Ahh," breathed her son, a hoarse wind deep in his chest.

Shussssh went the trees in Dulcy's grove.

STONE JUNGLE

Emily could feel the damp screen pimple her forehead as she peered down into the well of darkness between the buildings. The whoop, whoop of an ambulance passed by on the unseen street at the front of the apartment house, and she looked at the double-bolted door.

No one was forcing entry under cover of the mechanical shriek.

Ears still on guard duty, her eyes traced the descending line of bulbs on the fire escape opposite down into shadow-filled depths miasmic with old odors awakened by the autumn rain.

If she were in the dark, herself, she could see farther down.

Pulling the heavy flashlight from a drawer, Emily turned the kitchen light off, and sat, thumb on the switch of four batteries in a hefty black casing, listening to the distant chirp and wail of violated alarms from kids harvesting cars incautiously parked along the avenue.

There.

The girl, if it was a girl, rose out of the gloom, a white shadow among dark ones, vague and indistinct as mist from this height.

But she was there.

As she had been there the night before and perhaps for many nights, although last night had been the first time Emily had stayed so late at this viewless window, sleepless from the change of seasons in her own life, trying to plan her escape from this trap.

Stephen had stormed out of the apartment two days before, almost as soon as they had moved in, and Emily was slowly allowing herself to recognize that he had planned *this*. He'd meant to leave her in precisely these circumstances, with a month's rent paid yet a prisoner of the predators on the streets.

Emily had to admire the tidy quality of his requital.

She had packed their few belongings, withdrawn their money from the bank, done everything as he suggested, made cheerful by his apparent change of heart, his sudden willingness that they conserve their resources until they both could buy tickets and look for work outside the city.

They had no chance here, as they were.

City dwellers were either rich or modified and usually both. Their joint savings would cover only one partial body mod. Emily sighed, and rubbed her screen-roughened forehead. Stephen had decided modification was the way for him to go and once he had decided he had gone.

She had been stripped and abandoned.

The pale figure at the bottom of the well looked over its shoulder and crouched down beside an overturned garbage can—futilely furtive, for the white rags were too clean to blend with the mass of trash strewn over the floor of the pit.

Two tears rolled slowly down Emily's cheeks. She wiped them away, backhanded. She was done with that, as she was done with Stephen. Now what she needed to do was to make it through the long, uncertain night that followed the long, uncertain day.

Tomorrow she was going to have to find her way out.

Although this was where her husband had grown up, Emily had never lived in this part of the city. She was from the equally poor but less dangerous, because more dispersed, northern suburbs, where the school decks still worked, and every family had a vegetable patch squeezed into its bandanna-size back yard. She was a mark, here. Trapped prey.

Stephen's smiling face had hidden a lot of anger.

She had counted on his help in getting along until they could buy the two precious tickets that would carry them away from the city and out to where who they were and not where they were from might make a difference. Whatever the big deal was supposed to let him in on, it had seemed better than the deferred hope that was all she had had to offer—

Forehead stinging with the wire mesh, Emily saw a density, a thickening, in the blackness in the far corner. It moved forward a step and was unmistakably another ragged figure. This one dark and bulky as the first was pale and insubstantial.

The black figure struck the white.

A wordless scream echoed between the brick walls.

Shaking all over, Emily sprang back, looked around the barren kitchen, and returned to her post. Perhaps it was already over, a slap, a blow for some affront, nothing she need worry about.

"Oooo," came the wail, rising and falling as the dark arm rose and fell.

Even this high up she could hear the thud of fist on flesh. Emily looked around the four walls. There had not been time to install a phone, and even if she could reach them, the police might not come here.

She did not know any of her neighbors and from the padding of feet in the hall late at night, the hissing whispers of transactions at the door across the hall, she feared to unlatch her door.

There was a welcome silence.

Cheek checked by the screen, she leaned out, peered down. The white figure lay in its splash of fluttering rags. The black figure was nowhere to be seen. Hearing the thunder of her blood in her ears, Emily counted off long moments, waiting for some sign of consciousness, some sign of life.

Nothing.

There were rats in the recesses of the basement, and packs of wild dogs roamed the avenue when the packs of feral children modified only by disease and accident went home to their lairs. She leaned against the bulging screen. Crying out that someone should call for help would notify evil ears that she had no phone herself, and her bolted door would not withstand a determined attack.

She was new here, not yet reduced to total penury.

A small, dark form skittered across a white arm far below. There would be others, and soon, if the first was not driven back. Knuckles at her mouth, Emily listened. No feet brushed the mangy hall carpet. No alarms beeped and chattered on the avenue. Only the distant agony of a fire truck somewhere far distant broke the silence of the night.

She couldn't stop looking and she couldn't bear to watch and do nothing. *Act*, said a small voice at the back of her mind. *Act, or you'll be frozen here forever, remembering, and wish you had. After all*, it added, *no one would expect you to open the door now. You'll have the advantage of surprise. Do the good deed you'd want someone to—*

The hall stank of old urine and fresh vomit. She shouldered open the entrance to the fire tower, the unlit flashlight in her hand slimy with sweat. Turning and turning in the black gut of the building, alternately freezing at the movement of her shadow, then hastening on, too nervous to stand still, she climbed down five stories.

The unshielded bulb at the foot of the stairs was smashed and she turned on her light. The shifting oval briefly spotlit a cockroach, a brown smear on the squalid tiles, a little can of oil half-hidden by three parallel pipes. In daytime it would be in darkness. The old iron door to the well opened silently. Some-one came this way, often, and preferred that it be in secret.

Emily switched off her light.

The trash in the pit was in layers, like autumn leaves on a forest floor, and rank with trapped foulness. A hundred years from now, when the walls around it were cliffs of bricks and concrete where pigeons yet roosted, this place would smell evil still.

She could just see the white form, lying, outstretched.

There was no one, nothing, visible in the shadows.

Closer to, the supine figure seemed composed of wet papier-mâché. Emily thought, *Newspapers, she's covered herself with newspapers, for warmth, and the rain softened them, glued them to her clothes.* Flashlight in hand, she stooped, touched a gummy shoulder, began to ask—

The thing turned on its side and looked at her.

Its idiot eyes held nothing, not even fear.

Some subtle sound or current of air warned her to turn, flashlight swinging in an arc even before she knew her target. The heavy metal tube connected solidly with bone, jarring her arm back up to the shoulder. She swung again, and was not so lucky. The dark figure had moved back out of her reach.

Its breath hissed between its teeth.

Emily could smell old, wet feathers.

They maneuvered. When her back was to the door to the stairs, she backed away, one hand behind her, reaching for the knob and found cold metal. She tugged. It didn't yield. Terror shot through Emily. There was an automatic security lock.

She'd been stupid.

Stupidity kills.

In the instant of her distraction Emily's attacker had moved closer. She could smell it again, hear the hiss of its breath. It seemed draped in a great rustling cloak but it stank as if the covering were dirty fur or feathers. She shrank back.

It was the wrong move.

The cape whipped wide open, obscuring everything behind it, as the black figure clawed at her. Both her shoulders went numb. Tears streaming down her face, Emily knew that it would have her on its next pass. Her knees would not hold—

Then the door at her back opened, and a deep voice said, "What the—" and shoved her aside. She fell. Face inches from something stinking dead, she heard the dull explosion of a heavy caliber gun, once, twice. When the echoes stopped everything was absolutely silent.

"What're you doing here?"

Emily levered herself up, peered at her rescuer. If that was what he was. His action had been reflexive and self-defensive. Given the way things were, if a bullet in her head would solve a problem for him, he would shoot her, too.

She pointed wordlessly to the heap of white rags.

Beer belly bouncing, he walked over, prodded it with the toe of his boot.

Nothing happened.

"Is she dead?"

"She?" He chuckled, hitched his pants.

It was not a nice chuckle. It propelled Emily through the gap of the open door, and up the stairway as fast as she could climb, heedless of any listeners. Stupid, stupid, she'd been stupid, thinking if she did a good deed, things would work out for her—

She battered herself against the door to her floor, locked, from the inside, as security required it should be. Looking down into the dimly lit depths, she could see a bulky shadow turning its way up two flights below. Whoever he was, he was in no hurry, and she would bet he had keys.

With all her strength, Emily banged on the panel one more time. Then, as silently as she could, hugging the wall, she ran for the roof. She had no time to waste, she could feel the blood dripping from her fingers as she climbed and her stomach heaved with nausea.

If she went into shock, she'd be helpless.

The door to the roof opened with a press-bar, and she eased her way through as silently as she could, hoping that there would be something she could use to wedge it shut. But the expanse of gravel and tar surrounded by a knee-high parapet was bare of anything but the metal housings of the ventilation fans.

She could hide behind those, but not for long.

The door banged back, rubber foot dropping into place, holding it open.

He was grotesque. It hadn't been possible to really see that in the darkness at the bottom of the well, but now Emily saw he had been born ugly and had done his best to make himself horrific.

Feelers encircled his mouth, like the palps of some fleshy, outsize insect. One of his eyes had a faceted corrective lens grafted onto the surface, completely covering the iris. Both ears had been cut back smooth with his scalp. His knit shirt strained over augmented muscles.

It was not the look that made her guts knot with fear, but the knowledge of what it meant. Her pursuer believed he had transcended being merely human, and that those who had not chosen to evolve were evolution's losers, natural victims.

Emily felt hot little spurts of urine on her legs.

The palps twitched, smelling terror, and the mouth between them grinned. He was, she saw, prepared to take his time as he amused himself. She huddled, arms around her legs, dry mouth filled with pleas she knew better than to waste her breath on.

He reached for her, enjoying her horror.

Behind him, Emily saw the white figure rise on silent wings and land lightly on the parapet. In the gray light of false dawn no one would mistake it for anything remotely human. Whoever it had been, it now resembled a gigantic feathered bat, carbon-fiber-laced wings reaching out—

The thug was still grinning when the beast enfolded him.

Emily crouched, feeling blood run down her arms.

The captor's eyes closed, its sac of skin heaved and twitched, and then was still. It swayed and sighed in satisfaction as the last stars faded and a sheet of pale gray cloud was shredded into fleecy rags.

Somewhere near the horizon the first commuter flight droned up from the airport, a dark sliver against a growing band of primrose. The fathomless eyes opened, considered Emily. It could smell her bleeding. The great wings, their lining velvety with thousands of tiny tendrils, opened wide.

The bones that had been a man rattled as they spilled onto the roof.

The beast sprang into the air and was gone.

The grinning skull watched half dozen more flights rise be-

43

fore Emily could make herself sift through the heap of wet debris. The creature had left the man's keys, his knife, a nice handful of mixed change, three small plaques that looked like real gold, a zipper, and assorted buttons.

One gold would pay for a first-class modification.

Knife in her right hand, flashlight in her left, pockets stuffed with most of the rest of the loot, Emily crept down the fire tower, let herself onto her floor and into her apartment, shot the bolts behind her, one by one, and leaned back against the door.

Home.

She bent over and vomited.

Later, cold wet towels draped on wounded shoulders, and the spot on the floor findable only because it was so much cleaner than the rest, Emily considered going to the mod shops along the avenue and equipping herself with wings, poked her stacked coins carefully, frowned.

There was enough for a whole new life under her fingertips. She wasn't going to waste that, not even to enfold treacherous Stephen in the embrace he deserved. It was time to get out of the stone jungle, and if that required forgiveness, well, she could do that, too.

MOTHER TONGUE

I t had been there, at the corner of her vision, for several days, a dark fleck on the world, some tiny bit of debris knocked loose when she fell on the ice last Thursday. She tapped her papers into a neat stack and sighed. It kept its position in her field of view, no matter if she looked up or down or peeked sideways.

Frustrating, but a minor thing compared to finishing her book.

She picked up the title page, let her mouth silently shape the words, *The Rediscovery of Our Mother Tongue*, put it down again to stare out at the gray, dank day. Her work was based on simple observations, many that others had made before her.

But that was true of most discoveries. How many children had seen how neatly South America fitted into the coast of Africa before one man seriously considered the idea, and how many years passed before others refined and tested his theory? Yet now the whole story of the moving continents is known, and known to be true.

What she had found would be even more revolutionary.

She tapped her fingers on the pile of manuscript, remembering when she first knew what she had found. It was the code to the first language, the one that our ancestors spoke before they drifted apart into different tongues, cultures, and colors. Her reconstruction was far from complete. In fact, it was the merest beginning. It was enough, however, that the goal was in sight.

She smiled.

This published, computers would be loaded with every word known, comparisons made, original bases calculated, and the entire mother tongue recovered. United by a language embedded in the deepest structures of the brain, there would be few limits to what mankind, *humankind*, might accomplish.

A bus roared past the corner.

She looked up and saw the shadow in her own eye against the face of the clock. This evening, final proofreading, then the careful packing and the trip to the post office next day. She liked to make a bit of a ritual of sending off her books—

Abruptly, she really saw the time, and began to hurry, pulled on her coat, picked up her briefcase, went to face the thirty student faces waiting to be fed information. Making a mental note to ask about the fleck when she picked up her new sunglasses on Saturday, she shut the door a little too hard, and was off.

It was nearly dark when she got home. She was soaked by a cold rain that was going to turn to ice and then snow before the night was over. Toeing off her shoes, she shed her coat, her jacket, and propped her briefcase on the hall table. Stripped herself all the way into the shower, where she stood until the flesh of her toes crinkled.

Dinner baking in the oven, she wandered about, making the bed, straightening her makeup on the bathroom shelf, making a note to get an appointment at the hairdresser's, almost enjoying the tap of rain and sleet, and the groans of the wind-lashed trees.

She microwaved a cup of tea, she padded into her office to drink it, but avoided looking at the white block of paper dead center on her desk blotter. Not until she'd had dinner, relaxed a bit, cleared her mind completely so she could concentrate on the search for the misplaced comma, the word that was wrong for its context, the little errors that grammar and spellcheckers didn't spot.

She spooned the hot food out of its foil trays and onto a plate, something she normally didn't bother to do. One of those neglected little rules for surviving living alone: don't eat out of the pot; never sleep in an unmade bed; be sure your underwear is clean.

Rinsing the plate under the tap, she sighed. Foolishness. It was just the expected letdown after finishing a big piece of work, the moment when she could look around and see how many everyday things she had left undone. When the next project took her, she would be oblivious.

Nonetheless, she loaded the washer from the hamper.

By the time she was ready to take up the book, the rain had turned to the shuffle and hiss of icy snow, counterpoint to the hum of the washing machine. A quick check with the weather channel showed it was unlikely anyone would be going anywhere tomorrow.

She put her teacup in easy reach.

No reason to hurry, but the manuscript drew her, and pencil in hand, she began turning over the pages. She read top to bottom, back to front, having learned that let her see what was there rather than what she expected to see.

The wind moaned unintelligibly in the branches.

Crouched, naked, in the midst of a vast landscape of brown earth under a brooding sky, she knew it was a dream, although the ground under her toes had the texture of peat, and the air smelled of wet rock and storm. She was here to receive the gift of language.

She knew that, without knowing how she knew.

Drawing a circle around herself with her right great toe, she waited, arms up stretched, eyes closed, mouth open, tongue outthrust, feeling the words rush into her, like water filling a jug.

A hard gust of wind against the windows brought her awake with a start. Her mouth so parched her tongue felt swollen, she drank cold tea, stood, stretched, and drew the drapes closer together. She put the two blocks of paper, read and unread, on her desk, weighted them both against the flow of cold air from some unseen crack, and went upstairs. Bedtime.

She pulled the blanket over her shoulder, and slept.

It was a tower of square ramps, built of bricks brought by pilgrims, the poorest carrying only one or two, the richest bent forward under their loads. Thousands united in their desire to reach up to the sky and explore the secrets of the universe.

Disembodied, she flew over brilliant silver water and dull gold earth until she was on the rough, unfinished, topmost ramp high in the dark clouds, where thunder and lightening clashed. The wind tore at her hair, and she felt everything beneath her give way, and fell.

Until with a shudder she came to herself, and found she was standing beside her own bed, listening to the stormy night. *I'm obsessed*, she thought. She turned back the sweaty bedding, went to the bathroom, paced about a bit, putting distance between herself and the dream world.

Downstairs, one hand on each of the two pale blocks of manuscript on her desk, she stared unseeing at the folds of the drapes, feeling the raised letters on the laser-printed paper with her fingertips. The ultimate tragedy, that parting of the ways symbolized by the fall of the Tower of Babel. Soon, it would all change.

Struck by a realization, she straightened abruptly. She had thought of distinction but not of fame. One must give credit where it was due, but she intended to make it clear she was proud of what she'd done. So many old wrongs would be righted; so many others never come to pass. It would take time, but this was the first blow in the re-unification of mankind.

Humanity, she corrected herself.

It was quieter. She opened a crack between the drapes with one hand, contemplated the stark black and white, and closed them again. Tomorrow her creation would go out into the world. Meanwhile, she would lie in bed, listen to the sound of snow falling, and think of absolutely nothing until she slept again.

They wailed in wordless grief, the long lines of men and women robed and hooded in black. She saw no more of any of them than the occasional flash of a hand or the glint of light along a use-polished staff as they turned toward her, their silence condemnatory.

48

She knew who they were, storytellers, poets, historians—the lovers and users of words—mourning the death of all they had created. For all those worlds of words would die, as surely as some beast, its throat slit by the sacrificial knife, dies on the altar of gods unknown and unknowable to it. Their works would fade as their languages did, overwhelmed by the deeply rooted past.

The long line wound itself about her, every hooded head lowered, until on a great wail of wind, they looked where she crouched, naked, hands covering herself, and she saw there was only void where their faces should have been.

She screamed.

And woke to the pale light of dawn, stomach tight with wonder and terror, and went downstairs to package her manuscript with cardboard, tape, and self-sticking labels, safe with the babble of the weather report, ignoring the sliver of shadow in the corner of her sight. A small women, barefoot and in a bathrobe, about to change the world and careful not to think of it.

THE RAGGED MAN

Hearing the clash of spear on shield, I woke staring into thinning mist. One willow branch was battering another in a quickening breeze. It was a night much like the one when I lay down on the moss under the overarching ferns and died.

I was a soldier, once, a captain in my duke's personal guard when he took his army to Carneze. The city hadn't paid its imposts, and was letting peasants live within its walls as freemen.

The heralds demanded entrance. When the city gate stayed closed the engineers broke it in with the lesser ram. Our orders were to invest without looting. No pillage meant no profits, and the sullen infantry took their anger out on the townspeople.

I and my troop rode in together, ignoring the screaming, leaving the ordering of the foot soldiers to their own officers. The duke's guard got first pick when there were pickings and were paid to stay disciplined when there were not. Our objective was to secure the blackened keep that rose over the tile roofs of the houses.

The old builders had a knack of locking block on block so the stones themselves fail before the join, but they hadn't perfected a way of holding gates without men. We pushed our way past servants with poles and kitchen knives, rode over the beds of herbs and flowers, and dismounted at the door of the highest tower.

I went first. Up the stairs, into a room where the stink of potions and smokes hung heavy in the air. An age-twisted question mark of a man, bright-eyed and baleful, spread his arms to bar our way. Behind him, a veiled maiden caught up an iron-bound chest, fumbled to loose its hasp as she glided away.

"Back off," I said, drawing my blade.

His lips moved, "Accursed, unclean—"

I swung my sword.

"May you never die until—" My blade connected. His body slumped to the floor. His head bounced and came to rest among tumbled books and pots, mouth agape with astonishment.

I laughed, then yelled we must find the maiden. The troop surged in pursuit. The chest lay broken in the room beyond, but the bearer was nowhere to be found. I thought it some witch-thing, dead with its master.

We scoured the tower of defenders, then went down into Carneze, ate food from pots tended by weeping women, and went to sleep in beds whose owners lay heaped for the bone-fires. A day's work, less dangerous than most.

It was the dead hour between midnight and dawn when I woke knowing I hadn't heard the watch change. Naked, I slid from between the sheets, cracked the shutter and looked down into the moonlit square. There was no jingle of harness, no tramp of guards. Ashes and bloodstains lay waiting for rain to erase them.

Nothing alive, yet the shadows moved.

We had not found the witch-girl.

And the ironbound chest had been broken open—

I sprang down the stairway to the stables. Arms around the snorting horse's neck, I rode through a maze of courtyards, leaned into the darkness by the doorpost to undo the latch. A shadow reached up, clawed at my side. My steed screamed and fled into the street, taking me with him.

The city was dead.

Warriors lay slumped in doorways, sprawled in gutters. Near the broken city gate, the Duke himself lay in the mud, embraced by a darkness that snarled with blood-wet teeth. Foam flying from his flanks, my horse tried to outrun his own shadow.

The moon went down before the beast beneath me slowed to a walk, nuzzled in the trickle of water by a rock. Hand to my side, I half-slid, half-fell to the ground. There was a distant howling—wolves, or feral dogs. The horse mounted the bank in a shower of clods, snorted, and was gone.

All that fog-shrouded night I writhed, gripped by a cold burning. I saw fell things in every patch of darkness, but when the pain eased I slept, tired beyond fear.

I awoke, unable to move, staring at the red dawn sky. Gore crows came, sat watching. One thumped to the ground beside my head. I felt its feathers stir my hair, waited for it to dip its beak in my unblinking eye. One by one the carrion eaters pecked me painlessly, here, there, and flew away hungry.

Living things do not feast on the flesh of the undead.

I could not rot, but my unrenewed body frayed as wind and weather had their way with me. When the rain made tears in my hollow sockets I wept as if with rage. Bad luck to have been the first into conjurer's presence. Better luck that he had never finished speaking.

Dead men do neither good nor ill.

A passing fox clicked sharp teeth on my skull, hungry for the field mouse hiding within. Yellow leaves fell and covered my bare bones. A bellowing stag's hoof crushed finger joints. A burrowing beetle scattered others. I dozed beneath a blanket of snow and woke as bare as anything dead.

It was summer again, golden twilight. Puffing with effort, a round-faced boy climbed over the lip of the dell. He drank at the spring, ate a great slab of bread with cheese. Hidden in fern-shadow, I watched moonlit mice steal his breakfast while he slept.

The level rays of the rising sun shone on the spare curves of my cheeks when the boy's eyes opened. Eyes on the naked grin of my teeth, he backed away, his breath harsh in the silence. He scrambled up the bank, going back the way he had come.

I, a duke's man, had become a scarecrow for wayward children.

Icicles and new shoots, blossoms, fruit, and fallen leaves. I dreamed of old victories and warrior kings, woke to the heavy chink of harness, the squeak of leather on leather. The iron tang of anger filled my bony nostrils. Caught in the moonlight, the mounted horseman's mouth was a thin line of temper and will.

He backed the horse into the leafy cave beneath the willow, drew his sword in a whisper of sharp metal. The moon sank, the sun rose, the insect drone grew louder with the heat of the day, but he and his steed were one statue. Only the light ran up and down his blade a little as they breathed.

A hunter must have patience.

I heard them long before he did, although his ears were keen and the horse's keener. They clambered over the rim of the dell, eager for spring water and shade. Farmers, ignorant of the arts of war, deserting to do their first plowing. Churls, hardly worth a soldier's attention.

But he was no warrior.

There was a flash of light that had nothing to do with sunshine on steel. The peasants stood paralyzed. Their eyes glittered with terror as, one by one, the horseman carved their hearts out, spoke words of power, and sent the corpses marching back to his army.

You cannot kill the dead.

Meaning to wipe his blade, the spell-shaper backed his horse into the ferns. Under the leaf mold sticks and bones cracked. The animal stumbled as my skull rolled and was crushed under a hind hoof. In a jangle of harness, the rider fell. Reins trailing, the beast hobbled away on three legs.

The naked sword had been driven entirely through the man.

One hand to his wound, the spell-shaper raked the leaves with his free fingers, grinned bitterly when he saw my splintered cranium. "No living man—can defeat—me." Blood drooled from his mouth.

His fingers curled around the sword's hilt. A ripple of brilliance ran down the blade, but nothing more. His eyes rolled, refocused, and he reached out and gripped. Hand on a fragment of my skull he knew me for one of the undead and I knew he would have to end my bane to save himself.

His brows knotted with effort, the dying man's blood-slick fingers tightened. I willed myself to slip from his hand. Ferns rustled, a cloud-shadow slid across the grass, somewhere a hare thumped and was still—

I yielded.

"Be as you once were," he whispered. Hollow bone re-shaped itself beneath his hand. "Be as you once were." I felt my jaws clatter together, my teeth seek their sockets. "Be as you once were." My neck bones wriggled among the leaves, crawled on the ground, seeking the burden of my cranium—

Something broke in him. He died, snarling at the pain.

All day long the flies buzzed, busy at their feeding. The gore crows came, and the fox lurked, waiting for the birds to leave for the night. The field mouse stayed frozen with terror in its grass-lined hollow.

All night threads and rags of my flesh crawled to me, joined together. The dead man's spell, slow but sure, not swift enough to save him, nonetheless transformed me. Naked, whole, I woke to a clatter of spears on shields that was only the wind in the trees. I wrapped myself in the corpse's cloak and came away, leaving him to my wild companions.

I live on the charity of strangers, lady. If the story pleased you, a bite of bread would be welcome. A cup of milk if you can spare it. A man gets hungry when his bones wear flesh.

SUMMER-WITCH

S
ummer awoke, as she had awakened many times before, on the broad breast of the hill, the shattered remains of her brown husk around her, and the blue sky overhead. Her legs pointed down the hill, to the south, to the sun. She sat up.

To her left was the open grave of the spring-warlock, his head to the top of their hill, his legs to the east. To her right lay the grass-grown mound of their brother, the autumn-warlock of this domain. The fourth mound—that of their winter-witch, the sister whom Summer never saw—completed their circle of four.

Summer climbed out of her grave, stood tall, arms raised to the sky, stretching. Then she knelt and placed her hands on either side of Spring's sleeping face. So old, she thought, feeling the rough skin. Her brother's leaf-green eyes opened. He murmured, "Next year, my sister," and slipped back into dream.

All was well with him, then.

Summer swept the loose earth into his grave, patted it firmly into place, then sat back on her heels, and sighed. Some years the two of them were awake together during season-change. This would be a solitary year, for by the time her autumn brother awoke, she herself would be longing for the sheltering earth and the sleep of seasons.

Summer stood tall, and surveyed her domain.

Further south, other summer-witches had already awakened, and their rich green holdings rolled away to the hazy horizon, beyond which there were farms, villages, towns, and cities—places where the older ways had been bent to new purposes. Farther north, where the spring-warlocks had barely had time to bury their winter-sisters, the hills were still dun and drear.

When she came here again the northern hills would be red and orange with autumn, and the southern would be turning gold. By then her feet must have pressed every patch of soil, splashed through every stream; her hands must have caressed every plant, patted every animal. Feet drumming on the earth, the summer-witch began the long, sunwise spiral out from the heart-hill of her domain.

#

It had been foggy and the grassy slopes were slippery. *That was why I fell*, she thought, though she had never fallen before. It was not that many sun-turns since she had found this place and claimed it for her kin and herself. She was not old, not yet.

Hair hanging in strings before her face, Summer lay, tasting earth in her mouth. She was resting just a moment, listening to the roar of the brook at the foot of the hill, gathering strength. The wind shushed through the leaves, splattered her with larger drops.

It was going to rain hard.

One ankle was swelling, yet she must rise. If she did not dance, Autumn would stir in his sleep on the hill, rise early, try save the domain for their four. It was not even halfway through her season. Her brother would be weak, his renewal incomplete. He would fail. They would all die.

Summer staggered up.

Uphill was hard, but she topped the ridge, found a stick and moved carefully downhill, heading for the creek that flowed along the valley. Entering and leaving the water, the stream would carry her presence along its length, enable her to keep the domain's balance with the least possible effort.

Wind shook the groaning trees.

A big storm was gathering fast.

Water splashing about her feet, Summer danced as strongly as she could. The weakest summer-witch would have the coming turmoil deflected onto her domain by the others. It might take years before a major storm's damage would heal, and their four would be vulnerable while it did.

There were worse fates than simple death.

On her way north, so long ago, Summer had seen gale-stripped woods black and dripping with rot, ground erupting in foul masses of corruption, a danger to every youngling that passed. One such had come at her, eyeless, fingerless, grasping, seeking her life force to save itself and its kin.

The dying do not show mercy.

A wind-borne branch battered past her, lashed her with wet green leaves. Summer danced on, pain like lightening in her ankle. Through the screen of thrashing foliage, she could see a funnel, twisting about, seeking where it would strike. "Ahh, ahaaa," the summer-witch screamed, driving her terror out from within herself to ward it off.

"Oooooh," it breathed, and struck.

\#

Summer woke, chest pierced through by a jagged branch, groaned, pulled herself free, and fell senseless. Conscious again, she lay listening to her breath bubble and whistle, then rolled over and crawled downhill on hands and knees.

Not dead yet, she thought.

A bedraggled bird crouched on a rock at the edge of the creek. Summer reached out, touched him, watched it flutter up the bank and into the dripping underbrush. Her power was still with her.

If she could dance, she could heal herself.

Summer swayed, got to her feet, trying to establish a rhythm. If she made it to the outer boundary, she could restore her strength on midsummer's day. Striding on her knees, crawling on all fours, dragging herself forward by her fingers when she must, Summer spiraled outward.

No youngling could seize the domain while the four of them lived.

\#

The rap and clatter of hail filled the dark around her. Freak weather, which made Winter stir in her sleep, set the trees to shivering. Teeth locked on her lip, Summer stood still, listened.

"Oo, oo, oo, oo!" fluted something much too near.

A youngling, quest-calling.

A branch rolled under her foot, Summer slipped, fell into an explosion of pain. She thought, *I could just quit. Just stop.* The others would never know. Endings are as natural as beginnings.

"Oo, oo, oo," sang the voice, full of youth and longing, almost within reach.

Summer looked up into the determined yet callow face, and knew they both thought of her death. Eyes hard, they measured one another. The old summer-witch shifted a leg to ease the pain, and waited for the other to charge.

#

She was from near the edge of the cities where her kin had reared their pods for generations uncounted, shaping once-sterile earth and sky to the needs of creators so long-lost in the deeps of time they might be only legends.

Awakened to find she was surplus young, she had raced north ahead of the rest of her birth-cadre, seeking an undefended territory. Most who left the shelter of city edges died. Only the strong and lucky survived.

Summer could remember the first time she had come down the valley into this domain, her feet feeling the harsh, cold grass, her hair splattered with sunshine where the trees had not yet woven their canopy of leaves, hoping in every fiber of herself that this might be the place.

The old summer-witch had been on the top of the heart-hill, nothing but a woody skeleton with grass thrusting up through the slats of the ribcage. The elder must barely have made it from her grave before she died, face burned from the sun, flesh crumbling into earth.

Summer had spiked the remaining three of the old four with green, leafy branches. The stakes went in so easily that she wondered if the ancients had not already died in their mounds. She had feared the need to kill, was relieved it was done, that she had felt nothing.

How she had danced to claim her domain! Once, twice,

three times over every patch of ground, fingers caressing feathers, fur, hard chitin, scaly skin. When Autumn and Spring had carried the husk of their Winter north, she had been here, ready. None of them mentioned their wonder that she had succeeded where almost all of the cadre would have failed.

Summer had always been the strongest.

The younglings will have to pass me by, she thought. This year at least, I will not be a pale corpse in my green wood. Pain sweeping through her like fire, the summer-witch moved, insensible to anything but the need to survive.

Neck broken by a single blow, the charging youngling crumpled like a rotten branch and was as sweet in her mouth as fresh green twigs. The youngster had been foolish. Old, and wounded, Summer still knew a trick or three.

#

The sun stood high in the sky when she came to the boundary. With no time to spare, Summer sat, back against a tree, started to spin her thread of power. All through the longest day the summer-witches strove to bind the land in a protective net of force and she worked with them, substituting skill for strength, until she, too, was strong.

All through the short night that followed, Summer lay, eyes watching the circling of the stars as the land beneath her renewed her. When the sun turned the east rose and gold, the summer-witch began the long, anti-sunward spiral inward, the slow dance that begins the closing of the year.

When the day was no longer than the night, she came, feet drumming on the heart of her domain, up the hill, to kneel and open the autumn warlock's mound. Fingers cut by the fibers of his husk, she pressed her bleeding hand to his smooth forehead. He stirred, looked in her face.

Summer said, "You must wake and I must sleep."

"Yes," said the warlock.

Already her own husk was growing up Summer's neck. Soon it would close her lips, eyes, ears. Autumn took the summer-witch by her rough, thickening arm, lead her to her place. With quick strokes of his unmarked hands, he opened the turf so she could lie within.

She stretched out, feeling the healing earth surround her, closed her eyes as her brother closed her grave, sighed once, and slept again the sleep of seasons. Above her the wind lifted the first yellow leaves into a pale blue sky, blowing them away like forgotten years.

Sorcery

K em had lost the bar of soap again. Looking at the opaque, herb-littered water, he sighed, then hunted blindly under his thighs and around behind his hips with one hand. Nothing. He closed his eyes and leaned back against the smooth curve of the stone tub, feeling the spider-touches of the leaves and stems in the water with him. His head was one good, solid ache, the result of one or two, or perhaps even three, brandies too many the night before.

And Joseph's sleeping potion, of course—a bitter stew of herbs that was a cure almost as bad as the problem. Kem's stomach shuddered a little at memory of the black, fuming liquid. There was wormwood there, perhaps. Carenot. Seldren's rue. Only Joseph knew what else.

Kem had hoped a little plum brandy would calm him enough that he would get a night's rest. The fruity white liquor from the hills of Vaness had often sent him to sleep before when he was nervous. He had firmly thanked the old man for his offer to brew his specialty, but said he would do without the famous—or infamous—draught.

Joseph had concocted it anyway. It took three days to brew, and—as Joseph said, with a grim wisdom born of experience— "You might change your mind." Through two long nights the stench had filled the long halls of Fastness like impalpable dread.

By day, when Kem had kept to the mages' rooms where the dozen and more chimneys above the communal worktables kept the air clear, he had almost forgotten his worry in his study of his art. But at night the smell had been there to remind him, darkening even the shapes in his dreams.

The evening before the wind-eye's predicted appearance, Kem had paced and sipped one thumb-sized glass of the water-clear liquor, then another. When that didn't work, he sat down and drank more seriously. He tossed one of the small glasses to the back of his throat. Two. Then a third, sloppy full to the brim.

Then he had stopped: he would need all his wits about him tomorrow.

The first watch had passed as he listened to the clock chime the quarters, watched the man-shaped striker lift his mallet by jerky little increments and hit his tiny bell. When the last sliver of the moon set behind Fastness' outer wall, and Kem was still wide awake, he sighed and resigned himself, went to get the potion.

Joseph was decently silent.

The beaker the dose was in was fantastic work from the Isle of Pembry—a new-hatched dragonet writhing around the shell of its own egg. Back in his own room, Kem sat a moment, hands encircling the onyx base, admiring it. The cup's gold was painfully cold to the touch, frosted white even in the fire-warmed room, and a thin, pungent mist was forcing its way past the edge of the lid, falling over his hands.

Resolved to drink, Kem still waited. When a triplet of tiny hammer blows signaled the beginning of the second watch, he uncapped the beaker, and drank. The icy liquid sent a sharp pain through his teeth and skull. He gasped and swallowed the foul stuff as quickly as possible, trying not to taste what coated his tongue. Then he stumbled to bed, where he fell heavily asleep almost immediately.

He dreamed of Conred's death.

Trapped in sleep, Kem had tried again and again to change the course of events and failed. He remembered awakening, sweating and shaking with nightmare. Or perhaps he had dreamed that, too, for the view through his windows had been blood red with sunrise, and his room faced north.

The hours of the night had crept by, filled with remembered pain.

Finally the clock's mannequin struck his triple chime again, and Kem crawled willingly from his bed. His head was huge and tender, and his mouth tasted foul. Outside, the false dawn was gray and cold—ill omened, if you believed the village weather-wards.

He struck the wooden slit-drum outside his door once, feeling the sound throb through the bones of his skull. Two silent lower servants, faces pinched and wan in the lamp-light, came and went, filling the tub and bringing his breakfast on a tray. He got into the bath at once to escape their courtesies, soaking quietly until they were gone. They were willing to leave him to his thoughts. Kem was a rift-defender, mage, and rumored sorcerer—dangerous.

Kem moved his feet about restlessly in the water, feeling leaves and twigs brush his skin. Much as he dreaded the full daylight and the job ahead, his lips still twitched with annoyance at his shaking hands, even though trembling fingers were nothing new. He always suffered from nerves before a manifestation. Even before his first defense, Conred's death had taught him how fragile his, and everyone else's, safety was.

The rift was something that should not be. It sent the little hairs on the neck and the fragile tendrils of the mind quivering with its wrongness. It was wind and fire and a hunger out of nowhere, coming as the largest moon waned at the end of each month.

It took skill and luck to close the rift. Experienced mages sometimes failed and died. Inevitably, Kem thought, sometime in the future, the mages' defense would fail and everything would die, fast or slow, lucky or unlucky, burned like helpless scraps of paper by the ravening rift-fire.

Once or twice a week Kem robed himself and stood on the walls of Fastness, looking down at the traffic along the road far below him. He watched the country people on their way to the market, the townspeople on their way to their shops, envied their happy ignorance. Kem was guilty and glad he, at least, would be close enough when the defense failed that his agony would be one of the briefest—

The clock's mechanism gave a dull wooden tonk as some cog or gear shifted another notch toward full sunrise and the sixth hour. Kem started from his brown study, moved around in the water without really starting to bathe. He caught a leafy twig between his great and first toes, poked it clear of the surface in curiosity. Woebane. He could see the distinctive whorled clusters of the leaves. He dropped it back. The water was filled with steeping woebane, carefret, soris, and chumley. The four protective herbs.

Every mage bathed in this mixture before he robed and climbed to the high, stone platform at the top of the Tower. He could work in relative safety for however long it took until he closed the rift—or until he failed and another mage rushed up the spiral of stone stairs to take his place. Kem worked solo, but there was a triple of mages preparing themselves as his backup.

The rift had been a problem for generations. It had first appeared in the third cycle of the serpent, at Year's End, when the sun grew small and cold. It was almost nothing then, a tiny wind-eye of fire sucking the air into it in a growing storm. For a day or more it had been only an oddity. Then, as it grew larger and hungrier, its threat was perceived.

The earliest defenders had balanced, teetering, on ladders thrown together and bound by loops of rope at the top, then on hastily-erected wooden platforms dragged into place under them even as they strove, working as much out of curiosity as fear. Then one mage died, falling from the burning planks of his scaffolding. He never touched the earth.

Daltry—in those days mages had names—had been followed by four others before the rift was closed by two triples working in unison. Of the final six, three were never good for anything again. They had lived out their days, slack-jawed and drooling, in one or another chimney corner in the workroom, dead men who still breathed. The other three became servants.

When that first battle had been over, a huge hole had been

66

left—deeper than a two-story house, and wider than the town square. The sky was dark with unsettled dust. The mages cast the bones for omens and announced they feared another appearance in the next month.

Frightened, the townspeople began pulling the cobbles from their streets and dumping cartloads of the stones, one on the other, to fill the vast hole. Then the country people came with teams of oxen, hauling great boulders to the center of the field of cobbles. Everyone worked together to build a box of water-soaked timbers filled with stones—a crude, fireproofed platform—before the next manifestation.

And the wind-eye came again, larger than before, harder to control.

As the winter months went by, the able-bodied came from everywhere about to work for the common defense. Many of those too old, too young, too crippled for heavy labor came to make camp, cook, and carry what they could. Some few stayed home to mind the animals, and guard the storehouses.

The rift opened, as the mages predicted, three times while they worked, and those were the only days the people rested.

They surrounded that first rough heap with a mortared wall with an earthen ramp winding about it. They removed the timbers from around the boulders and hauled sledge-loads of gravel to the top, tumbled them in until the center of the stone cylinder was full of rock. A clay floor, brought up by the basket-load and pounded smooth by hundreds of bare feet, leveled the top.

Then everyone went home, exhausted, to make the goods needed for spring planting and sow the crops they would starve without.

The manifestations continued without pause.

Later, when the fall harvest was done, the people came again, paved the top of the Tower and the yard around it, and added steps to the ramp and faced it with stone. Although many careful hands had smoothed it over the years, the Tower still looked rough and wild, an act of desperation, a warning finger lifted in the center of an empty field.

No one lingered in the vicinity of the rift-bloom.

Even the youngest country children knew that when the mage had failed there had been nothing but a great hollow in the ground, that a hundred cartloads of earth, beams made from whole tree-trunks, and five men gone without leaving a trace to show they had ever existed. Their fathers cursed by the rift, and their mothers said the men were lucky they had no power.

The fiery wind-eye warped the world. The simple said that nightmares and their ghostly riders galloped through the opening, seeking out those helpless in their sleep. Mages said there was a quantifiable force, but they, too, faced horrors in their dreams—

As Kem had dreamed of Conred's death last night.

He moved his hands about in the water, searching for the errant soap without thinking. He felt the bar's ghostly touch and grabbed, but it slithered away again and he settled back, enervated by the warmth, the fragrance, his lack of sleep, and, most of all, by the need to clear his mind for what was to come.

Eyes closed, Kem concentrated—

Why had he dreamed of Conred now? Conred had never been part of Kem's rift-defenses. They had been juniors together, but Kem's first battle had been three weeks after his partner-to-be and best friend had died. That Conred was dead had nothing to do with Kem's exercising his own skills. He had nothing to fear.

Becoming a solitary mage was most often an act of arrogance, not necessity, but Kem had gone solo out of diffidence as much as anything else. When Conred had died, all the other juniors were already paired, and, although Kem was esteemed as a careful craftsman, no one asked him to be one of a triple— among the students the violently unpartnered were held to bring bad luck.

Kem had not been willing to ask anyone and confirm their

rejection. So he went to the rift-defense, his final trial as a junior and his first act as a mage, alone—and won. Strong and skilled, Kem had an honored place among the mages for his ability.

Still, because he had been too shy to seek other partners, Kem would spend the rest of his life working without another interlinked mind to protect him if he should tire and falter. He did not like to remember how lonely it was to face the thing of wind and fire that would wipe you out of existence without ever knowing you were there—

Kem pushed his thoughts away from the peril so soon to be confronted again, wriggled his toes in the cooling water, and wished this day were over. *No matter what the result*, he thought, and then frowned at the ill-omened thought. He might die, but the result always mattered—closing the rift kept their world in existence from month to month, and a rift-defender was the last to lack, no matter how hard the times.

But it was a privileged position dearly bought. The mages aged faster than ordinary men, and some years the wind-eye ate them like a fire burns tinder. There was a widely-accepted theory was that rift was the result of some sorcery somewhere other than this, that it swung into contact with their own world once a month, when their largest moon was just a fading sliver, because that was when the other world was closest to them.

Laughing Conred would have had some other theory, just to be different.

Kem and Conred had become fast friends at first meeting, in the manner of lonely young men who find someone like themselves for the first time, and strive to become like one another in every way.

They had walked and talked until their legs staggered and their throats were raw, and bore every moment spent apart only because it gave them something more to share when they were together again. The older juniors had smiled a little at them: it was the usual beginning of a good partnership.

Kem shoved the memories away, sighed and watched the small tidal wave echo off the sides of the tub. Then the pattern intersected his body and became only meaningless agitation, an ebb and flow of herbs and water. Finally everything was almost still again, barely stirred by his breathing.

He would have to be ready soon.

Kem still missed Conred, his quick warmth and easy banter, even his arrogant, carefree ways. "That's enough," Conred had said on many occasions, dismissing the careful rituals of the mages, and rushed off to complete some set task in half the allotted time.

Like the day they had been in the baths downstairs, cleansing themselves for their turn at the rift watch.

Though the times of appearance were precisely charted, the mages still maintained constant vigilance, and that duty was most often delegated to the younger juniors, hardening them to work outdoors in any weather, day or night.

The two of them had been preparing for an afternoon shift. Conred splashed himself all over under the inflow, then wrapped his threadbare, second-hand robe around himself, to stand watching while Kem scrubbed and scrubbed his skin to a raw pink, and rinsed ever part of his body three times as the rules prescribed.

Joseph was nearby in the leech's tank, simmering his aching joints in hot water and powdered woebane. He dourly watched Conred's scant cat-bath. "Make a better job of it," he said grimly. "You'll only fail once. The mages won't risk themselves to save you if you won't bother prepare yourself."

Kem involuntary made his village's sign against evil wishing. Juniors were not yet trained in true rift-defense, and the mages' speedy intervention was their only hope should there be an unexpected appearance.

Juniors' only weapons were the great iron bells mounted on the side of the tower, their clappers tied to lengths of chain that rift-watchers fastened around their waist so the bells would sound—and the chain stop their fall—if they leaped over the edge in panic. One or two young juniors had frightened one another into doing just that.

Fastness could not afford to lose any of those with power, even if they were too timid to do more than serve the mages— still, those who willfully put themselves into danger were not entitled to help from their fellows.

Joseph's warning was quite serious.

But Conred looked at Joseph's fire-scarred face, then at Kem's warding hand, then threw back his red-blond head and gave way to a gale of delight that made the old man glare at him in impotent fury.

Kem hastily toweled his shivering limbs, grinning at the floor in embarrassment. Conred might be his nearest friend, his partner-to-be, but Joseph had been a sober comfort to a raw country boy during the first long, hard days at Fastness.

In any case, mocking at one of the older juniors was un-heard of. Unthought-of. Most of what the mages-to-be learned was taught by word of mouth alone. There were few manu-scripts, fewer books, and no library at all. One's seniors had knowledge and had earned respect. Every step up the hierarchy was won by grueling study, often accomplished while in great peril.

Joseph's face had been burned while developing a more ef-fective warding spell. Left eye sealed closed with glossy white tissue, one ear burned away, maimed Joseph would never as-cend to magedom. One's senses must be perfect to wield power. But his defeat had been an honorable one, and he was a good teacher, a good servant to the mages.

And Conred had laughed at Joseph—

Kem's brow creased at the uncomfortable memory, and he pushed another small wave down the tub. It leaped and crested at the foot, showering the flagstones with its spray, raced back and slapped him in the chest. At little soothed by this display of feeling, Kem sank a little further into the blood-warm water,

71

felt the hollows behind his collarbones become pools, and closed his eyes to think.

He must clear his mind before he began the defense.

Conred had been quick and subtle, gifted with a flair for innovation that could sometimes make experienced mages wistful or envious, according to their temperament. The control they sweated weeks and months to acquire came easily to Conred. He put out his hand and power came to him, like well-trained hawk lighting on a gloved master hand.

Not an experience to engender caution in a bold young man, thought Kem, shifting his shoulders and feeling the water come and go. The tonks and clicks of the clock's mechanism sounded louder in the darkness behind his eyelids. Kem frowned, making deliberate haste in his thinking.

One by one Conred had dropped the protective practices the juniors were all taught. No one had argued with him. As long as he observed the precautions that protected the others in the Fastness, choosing his own methods was his right, however ill-advised his decisions. Wielding power was, after all, done through a personal relation with the universe, and ultimately each of the juniors must find his own path to become a mage.

Everything they did was dangerous.

Conred came to despise the accumulated wisdom of his seniors and the mages, and for a time, Kem, too, doubted. It was all so much simpler as Conred saw it. One did the minimum number of things to obtain the desired result. "Follow the straightaway," said Conred, and the road to power seemed to roll itself out before him, like new ribbon tumbling from a peddler's spool—

Kem lowered himself a bit more. Now the bath water lapped him under the chin with tiny sucking noises, and a flotsam of herbs drifted just beneath his nose. Soris, he thought in his private darkness, smelling the sour fragrance of spring hillsides. Kem put out his tongue, felt about and took the merest lick of a furry leaf. The pungent burn spread slowly, killing the foul taste in his mouth, fuming clean his sinuses.

He'd have to get out of the water soon.

Kem parted his lips and breathed deep, drawing the healing scent of herbs deep within himself. Mage Randel used a boiling pot with a towel to drape over his head for this part, like any village matron intent on improving her complexion, but Kem preferred the extra moments of solitude, of contemplation. Eyes still closed, he inhaled again.

Again and again Conred had stripped rituals to their barest bones and won through easily, unblemished, apparently immune to the minor burns and scorchings that beset his fellow students in their trial and error study.

That was when Conred began to argue with the older juniors, saying that his simpler rituals would be easier to teach, they could train more mages more quickly. Some listened. What the mages thought, they kept to themselves, but they made no move to stop Conred.

And, after all, why should the mages have cautioned him? thought Kem. If Conred's way had proved useful, that would have been everyone's good fortune. Fastness did need more mages. The rift pressed them harder every year, and the ranks of those who could win a rift-battle were thinned by death and misadventure faster than the mages could recruit and train the talented to replace the losses. Conred's bold simplifications might have saved all their lives, and he risked only his own.

Conred's luck, the first and second level juniors had called it as they scrubbed and meditated and conned long polysyllabic invocations that sometimes worked and sometimes didn't—and wished they had the nerve to cut short the grinding monotony and take Conred's way.

As good as Conred's luck, they all had said, meaning a thing was certain.

Yes, thought Kem, opening his eyes and sighing—a miniature gale that set the leaves and stems in the water sailing toward his feet—Conred's rebellion had been reasoned. He shifted in the water and the sailing tussocks of herbs fell apart in the waves. Kem closed his eyes again.

Finally Conred stood on the very verge of receiving his rod and being allowed to have pupils of his own—if any was reckless enough to take Conred as a teacher—nearly a decade before his fellows might hope to achieve teaching rank.

He had become very arrogant and even Kem, old friend and still officially partner-to-be, sometimes found him difficult to tolerate. Conred was like a man who walks confidently along the edge of an abyss because he does not know it is there, believes that it is not there for him.

Conred's former fellows plodded along, unwilling to deviate from the tried and true, and bore Conred's loud contempt of their failure to his methods in silence.

Until that day at supper.

Kem stirred uneasily in the cooling water, peeked and checked the position of the man with a hammer on the clock. There was still a little time to unravel this skein of thought. His dreams had been very vivid, and it was dangerous to face the rift with any distraction in your mind.

Or so it was assumed. Distraction was the reason given for why some experienced mages had wavered in the confrontation, then burned out of existence like straw in a fire. You must be very focused to defend against the rift, very balanced in your own mind. Kem closed his eyes and hunted for the dreamed memories.

There had been nearly two dozen men in the hall that evening, pale naked figures sitting on the cold stone benches in the gloom. Hungry, substantial ghosts, except for the two from the outer islands. They were so dark you could only see the gleam of their eyes and teeth in the flickering light from the hearth, or perhaps the disembodied shape of a pale palm and fingers as one of them reached for a serving dish.

Everyone had been talking of the day's labors, which had been mostly unsuccessful, as they always were. They spooned bean soup, chewed the hard bread from yesterday or even the day before's baking, and for all their professional conversation wondered silently when the first greens of spring would come from the south.

The great jars of salted vegetables were running low, and their late-winter diet was becoming monotonous as one item after another ran out. Onions, beans, and hard black bread were nourishing, but were delicacies only when contrasted with the alternative—starvation. At the end of winter even firewood was carefully counted out, stick by stick.

Conred and Kem were side by side at the far end of one bench, where they always sat lately, a little isolated from the others, as befitted their near-mage rank. Conred was talking, waving his empty spoon in the air to emphasize his points, ideas for new experiments pouring out of him in a torrent.

Kem had spent the afternoon standing in foaming water up to his shoulders while one of the hooded and masked mages shouted chants to test his theory that flowing water would offer protection from the smaller rift-like manifestations many of them could summon. Wendow wanted to be free to observe, and Kem was supposedly skilled enough to protect himself if the premise should prove false.

Kem spent the afternoon waiting for something to happen— nothing did. The mage had eventually snuffed the manifestation out, from, Kem suspected, boredom, and Kem had climbed out of the icy stream gray with cold, chilled through, ravenous, and shuddering, wishing the first mages had had the control that the simplest mage had now. Wendow had crushed the wind-eye between his fingers like a walnut.

In the hall, Kem helped himself to the soup, the bread, the honey-sweetened tea, only nodding whenever Conred paused in his monologue and seemed to require some response, smiling a little whenever his friend looked at him. The rest of the time he spooned soup and shoved bread into his mouth as fast as his hands could move, eyes on his bowl and the serving dishes, calculating how much he might get before the platters were empty. This time of year there was no snacking, no extra food. Not even a dried apple left the larder without the cook's approval, and Kem meant to spend a long night in the workroom, making up for the wasted afternoon.

If Kem had not been so self-absorbed, he might have told Conred to lower his voice so he wouldn't offend his fellows, irritable with failure and hunger and the raw cold that nipped their bare bodies. But he was paying less attention than usual to what his friend was saying.

Kem's lips twitched as he remembered that at the critical moment he had been fishing through the near-empty tureen with the ladle, thinking how unsatisfying it was that there was not even a scrap of meat in the soup, and how tired he was of salted salsify.

Conred, with no thoughts for what he was eating—stewed nettles would have done as well as white bean pottage—was telling the results of his latest attempts to refine the rituals to what he called "the aesthetic minimum"—nothing he hadn't said many times before.

But this time his emphatic voice filled a pause in the buzz of other conversations just when he was telling Kem that he could summon and control a manifestation without "any of that nonsense at all." Conred, as a junior, should not have been doing any such thing without a mage present as backup, and heads went up all along the long stone slab of the table.

Gan, who was for all Conred's successes, still the most senior of the non-teaching juniors, looked up. A bit of a butt for his methodical ways and unwillingness to complete the test that would give him his rod, he put down the loaf he was slicing, looked from face to face of his fellow juniors, and said, "Show us. If you can." The islanders grinned, white teeth gleaming in the gloom. One of them mouthed, *Now*.

Kem's spoon, halfway to his mouth, returned to his bowl with a tiny splash. Saying and doing were two different things.

He looked up to see Conred was the focus of attention. Some faces were grinning and others apprehensive, but none of them were friendly. Just the situation to put Conred on his mettle. The food turned to stones in Kem's belly.

A crease of annoyance on his forehead, Conred shrugged elegant disdain for superstitious riffraff, made a motion for Kem to continue eating, then reached for the bread and tore a bit off their loaf for himself, too sure of himself to be roused by such foolishness.

Gan said, "Unless, of course, you admit there's reason for caution."

It went so quiet Kem could hear the whisper of the flames licking the logs on the hearth. A stick shifted, popped. They all jumped and Jake's high, yipping laugh broke their silence. Then everyone but Gan, Conred and Kem tittered nervously.

Kem had already opened his mouth to deflect the conversation with some harmless pleasantry, when Conred said, "All right. I'll demonstrate." He dipped his bit of bread in the dregs of his soup very deliberately. "After I finish eating."

Remembering, Kem worked his tense shoulders against the cold back of the tub. The cooling water made hungry, sucking noises. Saturated, the herbs had settled to the bottom, where, presumably, the soap lurked too.

They had trooped down into the chilly vastness of the near-empty subcellars so Conred could prove what he said was true—at least for him. None of them truly believed that they could do things Conred did. Conred was special. Traditions, hard-won knowledge, were all that kept the rest of them alive.

And, for all the talk about Conred's luck, they were still pale with apprehension. Being too close to an uncontrolled manifestation was dangerous. Conred's summoning one would be a clear violation of the rules, but no one had the nerve to go for a mage. Or even to say what they were doing was foolish, that the matter would wait for some better day or future test.

No, they had all huddled together like goats in a pen, watching as Conred, who stood alone on the cracked flags in the center of the stone floor, raised his arms and began—without any preliminaries at all. No wardings, no exercises to focus the mind, nothing.

The startled herd of students gasped and backed against the wall, frightened, held there simply because each was unwilling to be the first to leave. Kem remembered how hard his heart had been beating, as if it wanted to leap out of his chest and run away on its own, since Kem was too foolish to seek safety.

He had slowly backed his way up the stairway until he saw the whole scene spread out beneath him as if he stood on a cliff, removed from the turmoil of the waves. Then he either lost or gained his nerve, broke, and ran to the forbidden upper halls to summon the mages, intent on saving Conred from himself.

Kem sighed, alone in his cooling tub. He had not seen the rest, only heard it described so many times he could recite each witness' version.

At first there was only Conred, mouth filled with words, muttering to the air like any traveling actor pretending to be a mage for some penny-paying audience of yokels. Then the air thickened and grew dense, and the tiny sounds in the vault grew loud and threatening.

The other students flattened themselves against the wall, feeling the silent wave of power driving toward this shore from somewhere else. They all smelled the smoke of the manifestation an instant before it appeared. It hit, exploding into this reality, a swirling knot of air bigger than a man's body, a fume and froth of—

Fire.

Someone screamed. They all turned to run and found each other in the way, trampled one another to reach the stone stairs. Only Gan held his place, watching. He said he saw the flames "blossom like a summer rose." Then the heavy air shook with an astonished scream. Conred was engulfed and gone before

Gan even thought to mutter a syllable or two of warding.

Conred's luck had failed him.

Roused by Kem's frantic appeal, the mages robed and came to investigate, in what seemed no great hurry. They paced down the stairs to the subcellar in their couples and threes, sniffed the air, looked at the broken and scarred floor that was just as it was before Conred began his summoning.

"A great loss," one said, tapping a gloved forefinger against his mask, perhaps where his lower lip was.

"Just as well, perhaps," another said, tartly, giving the bleating huddle of students a searching inspection through his slanting eye holes. The mages did not lower their veils when they were indoors and not working. He got a sharp look from the first and said no more.

There had been no body to recover, although the floor was swept reverently, and the result cast to the winds and the tides as was the custom for a burned body, along with a bucketful of ashes from paper offerings lighted for Conred's spirit. The mages did not believe in the rituals, but Conred, like most of them, had come from simple country people.

Kem sighed again at the memory of the gray and empty waves pounding at the seawall. The water in the cold tub was growing chilly. He opened his eyes and looked around his barren cell, furnished almost entirely in stone. It was unwise to keep much that would burn near a mage, and manuscripts and papers were useless. Anything written must cut in metal, drawn in clay and baked, or engraved on slate, and sometimes even these failed.

The craft must be carried in the mind.

So the room had only a tub, hollowed from a piece of stone, and another block of rock that served as table or invocation altar. There were a few tools in jars and jugs: binding cords, firerods, and bunches of herbs, mostly. The bed platform was built from the granite of the floor itself, and covered with deliberately scanty bedding of well-tanned leather.

By the hearth was Kem's single indulgence, a three-legged low wooden storyteller's chair, ornately carved and painted in the manner of Terrenforge, his home village. A present from old friends when he became a mage, it provided the only touch of color in the black and gray room. Its uprights and back were covered with yellow, blue, and green lozenges filled with the tiny figures of Fellsen country art, men herding sheep and cattle, women grinding grain and gardening. The seat, worn blurry with use, was a brilliant emerald figured with a blue and turquoise pattern.

The dark, hooded robe Kem wore in public and before the juniors was by the bed, draped over its stand—a single, upright slab of rock with sloping shoulders and a vestigial neck. The mask, veil, and gloves lay in the litter on his worktable. The boots were by his chair. They were the only garments he owned, for otherwise he went naked, whatever the weather. Clothes often burned in the presence of mages. Like bedding. Like books. Like letters.

Kem closed his eyes again. He did not precisely grudge his efforts, but he found life as a mage lonely. He had grown up in the hustle and bustle of country life, where the heartbeat of the seasons seemed to bind the whole village together into a balanced whole. There were still moments when he wished he were not talented, that he had been away from Terrenforge, herding or hunting, when the examiners came.

That he had not become a mage. That he at least had a partner in his work. Sorcerers, solitary mages were called, not entirely in jest, for they wielded greater power than their conjoined fellows, took greater risks, failed more spectacularly. Were more often envied. More often hated—

A dangerous, self-indulgent line of thought.

Kem forced himself to concentrate on the present, sitting up in the cold water with a slosh and hunting around him with more vigor for the soap. He needed to make himself completely ready before the sun rose, and the clock on the table was close to the sixth hour, the manikin nearly ready to strike.

Where was the soap?

Kem sighed and absently muttered the least finding-spell, the first he'd ever learned. Nothing happened. Then he scowled and made an explicit, rude gesture. The bar leaped from the water, fell back—splashing his face with soapy water—and vanished into the depths of the tub.

He rubbed his stinging eyes and grumbled a common, ineffective curse. Worry and late drinking had clouded his wits. The soap was supposed to be resistant to spells. He hoped he'd not impaired its efficiency with the illward's charm. He was a mage, able to see and seek, without calling on anything beyond himself.

Kem closed his eyes—hunting for the essence of powdered touch-me-not and woebane, lye, and animal fat—reached down into the water quite deliberately and closed his hand around the bar.

He began lathering a stiff-bristled brush. The block was slow to foam, being composed more of herbs than good, honest soap, but he rubbed grimly, nonetheless, until he got a brushful of suds. He began, methodically, to wash, starting with the little toe of his left foot, muttering the wardings as he worked.

He scrubbed all over, left side first, bottom to top, careful to see that every part was coated twice and rinsed, and rinsed again. When he was finished, islands and peninsulas of foam floated in the cloudy water and he was the familiar raw, bright pink. Kem could tell he had been thorough. Every inch of skin was stinging.

He got out of the tub, stood on the pierced grate by the outer wall. The cold iron bit his wet, naked feet as Kem pulled the knotted rope that hung there. Gallons of icy cold water from the cistern on the roof cascaded over him. He lifted his face to be battered by the water, turning his arms one way and then the other under the flood, scooping water over his less exposed parts, directing the flow over his hips and crouch.

Scoured and drenched clean, Kem took the huge, coarse towel that lay folded on a stone shelf. He huddled himself into it, hooding his head and wrapping it around his body, in a casual semblance of his robe. Padding to the stone table where a tray with a beaker of water and a single covered dish waited for him, his stomach shriveled to a knot of apprehension. He hardly wanted to eat, and yet he must.

If events went against him, he might strive for a watch or more.

He lifted the pottery cover, and the smell of burned toast filled his nostrils. Kem frowned and suddenly looked like the man of powers that he was. If he hadn't asked for much there was still no reason why it should not be appetizing.

The two pieces of scorched black bread, innocent even of butter, lay curled side by side in the dish, like the soles of some outworn pair of boots discarded in a hedgerow. Next to them in the shallow brown bowl was a single pale, salted root. A parsnip, thought Kem, prodding its gritty limpness and licking the salt off his fingertip. He particularly disliked parsnips. It was as unpleasant a meal as he had ever seriously considered eating for non-magical purposes.

He raised a hand and wearily did a small transformation spell.

The toast and parsnip disappeared and a puddle of gray gruel appeared instead. He lifted the bowl, scooped a hot mouthful with two fingers—like any hungry village cowherd in a hurry to milk his mooing, restless animals. He was reluctant to waste any power on making a spoon, or any time on the nicety of opening his door, sounding the wooden drum, and sending a servant for one.

Although the porridge still smelled faintly of scorched bread—perhaps the dish held the odor—it was edible. It was what he had eaten when he was still a boy, and it should do as well today. Poverty's food at the end of winter, unseasoned even with salt—Terrenforge was that far inland.

Kem scraped the dish with his thumb, licked it clean, and turned the cover upside down in the dish, wondering if anyone in the kitchen would notice they'd sent up toast and gotten back a bowl sticky with gruel.

Probably not, for if Poud had been supervising the kitchen, he would have seen the toast was not burned, and there would have been hard red cheese, and—despite the time of year—butter, and honey-sweetened lime tea.

The cook knew someone up this early was likely to be a defender, but to whoever had the night watch in the kitchen, Kem had been a nuisance using mage's authority to ask for a snack, just someone to be discouraged from making inconvenient requests with a little bad service.

One more little problem to be dealt with when Kem finished his rift-battle.

The mages did not tell whom they had summoned for the day's defense to anyone. The masks, hoods, and veils preserved their anonymity beyond their own small circle and their few trusted servants, who were mostly failed juniors or maimed mages.

Kem washed his hands past the wrists again with the dark brown soap, paring under the nails and rinsing the ritual three times—and once more for luck. The faint lingering scent of scorch in his nose hardly mattered, he'd be smelling enough of that soon. Still, he cleansed his mouth with cold water, once, twice, three times, cleared his throat and spat, and did the whole thing again. Finally he brushed his damp hair into order, clipped it at the nape with a clasp of human bone.

Be with me, he thought, head bowed. Seldren had been a friend.

He stood a moment, naked, clearing his mind of any thought beyond his duty, then donned his dull, lackluster robe. His mask crinkled and his gloves rustled as he put them on. Despite the fire, the thin-soled boots were icy from the chill breeze down the chimney and his feet cringed as he forced them in.

It would soon be time for a new pair. Another trip or two to the Tower and these would be worn enough to be given to some new junior for his first or second pair. That would come soon enough. Today Kem wanted the comfort of old, tested things protecting his body.

The robe slowly brightened until it shimmered and flickered with vague, indefinite figures of flame. He raised his hood over his head, dropped the veil that protected his eye holes. Now he was no one, everymage. If he failed today, no one would know that it was Kem of Terrenforge that died. No one would curse his name, his family, or his village.

He stood on the hearth before the seven-spoked wheel of fate carved in the wall above the fire, raised his arms and prepared to invoke his powers. He took a last, slow breath before beginning. Do it wrong, and the servants would find a blasted hulk on the stones when they came to escort him to the rift-defense.

He closed his eyes for concentration—his masters had always condemned this habit of excluding the outside world but there was no one here to see—emptied his mind of any extraneous thought and began.

He shivered once, then barely breathed, counting each slowing breath.

It started as a numbness in his hands and wrists and poured slowly into his body, filling him as a jug is filled with spring water so cold it hurts to hold the pot in your hands. At each moment he thought the pain was too great to bear and then learned that there was another level of agony he had not remembered, yet must once again endure. The pain went on and on—

He felt his heart stop.

He floated above the earth, seamed with rivers and patched with seas, seeing the green lands of the farms and the deeper green of the forest, the pale green of the grasslands that rippled like a sea. He felt the swelling force within himself, saw the livid fury leap from the earth to him and back, ripping the air apart, summoning his power, binding him, making him one with the elements, cold and wet, heavy with rain and pricked by lightening. His human ears heard the rumble of thunder out of season over Fastness and he lowered his hands.

He was Cloudmaster.

His secret name, that he had never told anyone, not father, not mother, not lover, not Conred. Cloudmaster. Filled with the power of the seas and earth itself, prepared to face the other two elements, the wind and fire of the rifts.

He opened his eyes and looked around him with the queer, bleached vision of his mage-sight. He flexed his gloved hands before him, bound his robe more closely about himself, felt that the edges of his mask were in place, his hood well forward, the veil secure.

The mage was ready.

He opened the door, took the stick hanging beside the wooden drum, struck a single solemn note, and almost heard the scuffle of his servants' running feet.

It was the time.

#

She had been waiting a long time in the crowd, restless with excitement, and perhaps a little fear. They all said it was perfectly safe, that the thing, whatever it was, struck only at the mage and that he would defend himself. If he failed, another would take his place, and so on until the thing wearied and died away for another month.

That it was a year's good luck to see the thing done.

It was really quite safe.

The mage appeared, a solitary, spare, smoky figure unhurriedly climbing the stairs that spiraled the tower, as if the danger would wait for his coming.

Rosinel saw as he came around the spire of stone again, already higher than the tallest house in the town that he was, he had been, quite a tall man. The anonymity of the robe and mask could not conceal that he was tall, as the men of her own village often were. She wished him well for that and missed the beginning of the chant.

Her nearest neighbor nudged her rudely in the ribs and Rosinel raised her high, clear voice, easy to hear among the rest. The massed sound was rich and sustaining, and yet she felt her well-wishing might have done the mage as much good as the old invocation with its forgotten words worn formless and soft with repetition.

At the top of the Tower, the dark figure stood, head down— like any tired man pausing in the day's work—and waited.

She thought, *He might once have been a boy in my village, feet filthy with dung like any other cowherd.* Just another boy, laughing and running through green spring, golden summer, red autumn, and the white cold of winter. He'd have had one or other eye always just blacked by someone's fist and his knuckles fresh-cut by someone else's teeth. Now he was no man, greater—and less—than any child born of woman. The mages were said to be reborn, of their own will, in the fiery womb in the sky.

You had to die to be a mage.

Rosinel willed hope into her voice, shaking with sudden terror that he might fail—

#

He could smell burned meat and blood and there was a taste of iron in his mouth. The knot of gloves in his left hand was a total ruin, every finger split to the palm. A new pair would have to be made. One sleeve of his robe was singed to feathery rags. The new one would have to be woven with fresh spells, since the old wardings had failed. That seemed very important somehow.

New wardings. Fresh spells. Sorcery.

The mage sat down heavily on the chair by the hearth, dropped the gloves to the floor. He loosened his robe and let it slide into a pool of cloth around his hips, then toed off his boots. Kem sat, elbows on knees, one hand rasping the stubble on his chin, too tired to even consider entering the steaming bath that sat waiting, or lifting the covers of the numerous small dishes that leaked steam and fragrance on the tray on his table.

It had been a hard fight against the flood of heat and fire that sprang into being around him. The burning brightness was filled with the half-seen forms of things that walked like men and were not, might not even truly be there, be only the imaginings of his startled brain, pictures like those a man may see in the coals when the fire burns low.

He had seen Conred's imploring face again, felt ghost hands pluck at his wrists.

He had been wrapped in fire and drowned it with the force of water, lifted by wind and stopped it with the power of solid earth. And slowly, painfully, he had won. Won them all a month's respite, then fallen to his knees on the Tower's stones as his heart stuttered back to life and shook his cold, shuddering body with its renewed beat.

Between two of the attending mages, he had even walked away with dignity, slowly down the stairs he had climbed so easily, so deliberately, vaguely aware of a roaring that must be the foolish crowd, not the all-consuming flames.

Once they reached his room, he had waved away the helping hands, wanting only solitude in his weakness. And now he was here, alone, safe, unscarred, duty done for many months.

Kem staggered to the bed and fell, face down. Only a man again, mind numb except for the refrains that filled his head, waking and dreaming, the endless mourning for his friend and the regret that he had been so slow to understand. That he, Cloudmaster, had the power by his very presence to defeat wind and fire.

That he alone had always been Conred's luck.

GREENWIFE

The crow that had been following the only moving thing in the white landscape cawed once and flew on, straight toward the horizon. I turned the wheel, felt my car slither until its wheels bounced back into the furrows ploughed by earlier travelers. Three miles to Three Corners. I could stop and think about whether to go on when I got there. Right now the road required all my attention.

I was already past the van left nose-down in the ditch when the driver's door popped open. A bundled figure scrambled into the road and waved both arms vigorously. I took my foot off the accelerator, rolled slowly to a stop.

The anxious face that peered through my side window was dark and rough with beard. I bit my lip. In ordinary circumstances I would have refused to let a strange man in. Today, with the temperature in the single digits, ordinary caution was first cousin to murder.

I popped the lock, and he joined me, bringing a blast of Arctic air with him.

"I'm Jeff Kourahan," he said, pulling down his scarf to give me a good look at him. "I appreciate your stopping."

"Cindy," I said, setting the car slowly into motion again. "Cynthia Appledon."

"The old lady's daughter," he said, rubbing his hairy cheeks. "People wondered," Jeff paused, "why you hadn't come." He looked out his window. I wouldn't have picked him for a local. His knit cap, scarf, and quilted coat were what everyone wore, but obviously new.

"I was out of the country," I said shortly. "On business." In Greece, to be precise, leading a group of tourists around the ancient sites, telling new versions of old stories, and arguing with bus drivers and hotel desk clerks.

He nodded, well-I-knew-that, and I suppressed a spurt of annoyance. Three Corners is a small place, without too many secrets. The sole proprietor of Classic Tours, Inc., I come home twice a year for a month or so, travel the ancient world the rest of the time. It's a good living, and advance compensation for—

The car hit an icier patch, slued. I turned the wheels, tapped the accelerator and recovered. At Three Corners, a church, a store, and a half-dozen houses at a "y" in the road, I crunched to a stop in front of Barney's General Purpose. Tourists find Barney's quaint. Natives know its tight-packed clutter is born of necessity. There are no quick trips to Championberg once the winter sets in. The store has a public phone.

Hand on the door latch, Jeff cocked his head at me, weighing his words. "I've taken the house a quarter mile beyond your mother's. I'd save me a good deal of trouble if you just take me on." Our taxi service is intermittent. Jack Chauvenet doesn't like to turn out in bad weather.

I put my hands at ten and two on the wheel. A quarter mile beyond my mother's meant he'd rented Stone House. If Tom Wheeler trusted him with his property, Kourahan was trustworthy indeed. Wheelers are cautious to a fault, have been for two hundred years and more. I shrugged, set the car rolling again, past the white wood columns of the village church.

"Thanks," Jeff said, then, hesitant, "You may not have heard. I've been doing a little dairying. Come May, I'll be opening a shop for the summer trade. I'm up here getting the new nannies settled, going over the place."

He was milking goats. I nodded, mind mostly on the car's uneasy motion, remembering a black kid climbing an olive tree, disks of sunlight dancing on twig-littered ground, a sharp, feral scent. There'd been a distant clamor on the breeze, a dog barking and someone beating on a pan.

"I've named it 'The Greenwife.'"

Startled, I glanced at him, but he was lost in his own vision of herbed cheeses and happy tourists, a hand-carved sign and a steady trade with the New York gourmet stores. Coaxing the car up Henderson's Hill, I bit my lip thoughtfully. Jeff's woman of wooden leaves, flowers, and fruit was not—

"Look," the male voice said softly.

Caught in the level sunbeams, the icy maples at the crest were a glory of ebony, crystal, and gold. I drove straight into the glare, trusting my memory that the road did not curve until the foot of the hill. Jeff twisted to look back, but I didn't dare glance in the rearview mirror as the car slithered in the ruts.

The snow was pink in the evening sun's light, lavender in the shadows, when I turned into my mother's drive and stopped short. Jeff would have to walk from here. The car would never make the long slope to Stone House. He gathered himself together, put his hand on the door handle, said, "Shovel your walk?"

I nodded yes. I'd picked my clothes for the plane and the city. My high-heeled boots would make it awkward getting to the snow shovel that leaned beside the mailbox in the closed porch, and my thin gloves would be a complete loss after five minutes' work.

He got out, and I switched off the engine and pulled the lapels of my coat across. They sold gas at Three Corners, but this time of year it was hard for the truck to come. I must not waste what I had. There was no telling if my mother had laid in her winter supplies. There were a few items that always required a trip to Championberg and she didn't get around anymore.

I rolled one cold shoulder and then the other, trying to ignore the steady scrap of metal on icy stone, the fact that there was nothing but frost at the window panes. Just this summer Mother's curious, welcoming face would have peered out as soon as any car pulled into the drive.

When Jeff stashed the shovel on the porch and came over, I lowered my window, and said, "Thanks."

"Want me to wait while you check things out?"

I shook my head. "It'll be dark soon. You should be getting home." I knew what I was going to find. I wanted to be alone with it.

He squinted at me, mouth full of unasked questions, then decided to take me at my word.

"Thanks," I said again, for that, and for the cleared path.

"Welcome," he said, having already picked up the sparse local conversational style. He strode away, not hasty but making good time, a broad-shouldered figure with a giant's shadow.

I rolled the car window up. Probably on his way to a warm supper prepared by a wife or girlfriend newly-elevated to business partner. My breath blurred him out of existence, even as I imagined what the woman must be like. Short and dark, with fake tortoiseshell earrings and a husky laugh, or tall and blond in a pale blue sweater—

I looked at the silent house while the frost grew feathers and needles across the windshield. The car ticked, cooling. I hitched my coat tighter around me, watching the few clouds fleeing west turn ruddy then ashen. The wind was rising. By morning the autumn's first snow would look new-fallen again.

When two or three stars appeared on the eastern horizon, I got out cautiously, slid the slick soles of my boots along the walk. I could freeze to death if I fell out here. The bare-limbed bushes chattered in a gust of wind as I eased myself up the steps. The sheltered porch seemed almost warm as I fished my spare house key from my purse.

Half a dozen humidifiers sat purring on the living room floor. Mother must have arranged for someone trustworthy to come in and refill them, check the furnace, do what little needed to be done for her. I'd have to find out who. They'd have a key to the house I'd need to reclaim. I unwound my scarf, unbuttoned my coat, hung both on empty pegs in the entryway, and then left my foolish boots leaning one against the other.

I looked in every room as I passed, stockinged feet padding on the bare boards. The house looked unoccupied, rugs rolled up, furniture covered. All the windows were blind with frost. I called, "Mother?" and heard my voice whisper back from dusty corners. A mouse, driven in by the cold, fled under a bureau, peered out with beady eyes.

Unlatching the door to the back hall, I stopped. At the far end chipped stone posts framed a rectangle of total blackness. A cold breath of mold touched my face. It took an effort to move to the gaping hole and look in. "Mother?" I switched on the lights. The great tree rooted deep in the earthen floor didn't even rustle.

She'd settled in well. Already it took a sharp eye to see the human form in the trunk and upraised branches. The bole that had been a face was healed over, closed, its nostrils, mouth, and eyes stopped forever. There would be some consciousness still. Grandmother's apple-blossom hair quivered with muffled song days before her daughter went to walk the hills, singing in the spring.

I looked up at the shuttered skylight, sat down on the step formed by the end of the flooring. An ancient tune droned in my head as I tried to think. Tomorrow, or maybe the next day, I would check the arrangements for the house. I had twenty, twenty-five, possibly thirty years until my own greening.

The furnace switched on with a rumble.

I drove my nails into the palm of my hand.

It was not fair, the loss—of freedom, of ordinary pleasures, of my *self*. I reached down and pressed my bleeding flesh against the cold soil of the winter room, remembering rocky hills and bold blue seas, doomed fish glittering in the net, and a whiff of laurel on the wind.

At the end of summer the whole house would have smelled of dry grass and sun-baked dust. Naked, her beautiful hair flowing past the narrow waist that childbirth hadn't taken from her, Mother had come here and embraced the tree, serenely confident that I would come home, tend the tree and wait my turn.

I pressed my stocking-covered toes into the cool, crumbling earth. The local legends call us greenwives. "A simple corruption of 'goodwife,' one tourist had told me, and I had nodded and smiled polite agreement. It was hard to imagine—

"Cindy? Ms. Appledon?" I hadn't paid much attention to him, but I certainly knew the muffled voice. Jeff Kourahan. I staggered as I stood. I must not have relocked the front door. "Jeff?" Feet thudding on bare boards, I ran to intercept him. "What are you doing here?"

Key in hand, he stood in the entryway. Seeing my anger, he flushed. "I thought you might need some company, or at least some dinner." He offered the heavy bag in the crook of his arm. "I did say I'd been looking after things."

"Oh," I said, deflated. Busy with driving and my own thoughts, I'd missed that. I fumbled for some way to depreciate my anger without losing moral ground. "You should have knocked."

"I did. Hard. Several times."

"Oh," I said again. Then, expecting him to apologize, "You startled me."

His jaw lifted a stubborn fraction. I said abruptly, "Go into the kitchen. I'll be right along." Hands shaking, I closed the door to the back hall, carefully shutting in the cold, moldy smell. Perhaps Mother had simply told him she was going away for a bit and asked him to care for things.

Perhaps not. I licked blood and earth from my palm. My mother had always been discreet, but when you green you are in the grip of uncontrollable needs. If Mother had said or shown too much—I pressed my hand to my quivering lips. She should have sent for me. I would have come. I'd told her that.

I walked into the kitchen just as Jeff turned the overhead light on. Row after row, jewel-like, preserves filled the shelves around the walls. I could count the days and weeks before Mother's greening. There were no pears, no apples. This autumn the birds would have eaten their fill in our trees and the deer feasted on windfalls.

Jeff piled his coat, hat, and gloves on the table beside his sack, lifted out a bottle of wine, a cloth-wrapped cheese. There was dark, curling hair at the neck of his shirt, and I could smell his musky maleness. I stood, blind and deaf, trying to think of a way to ask how much he had seen, what he knew.

"Cynthia?" A dark-nailed hand, gentle but firm, lifted my chin. I stared. Jeff was a handsome man, with black eyes and a proud, curving nose, but that was not what drew my eyes. Above the smooth sweep of his forehead, among the curls pressed flat by his knitted hat, there were twin knobs of horn.

Silently, he laughed at the round "o" of my mouth.

I turned to flee, my heart filled with the proper joyous terror.

He held me in place with his free hand on my shoulder. "Once more," he said, giving me a little shake, making sure of my attention, "have you got any wineglasses?"

"In there," I said, pointing with a glance.

He released me.

I stared at tear-blurred purple plums and golden apricots, thinking of one hot noon when I crouched in the shade of a marble pillar. I had wanted to believe that someone was hiding in the shifting shadows, safe from merely human vision, but I knew there was no one there and never would be.

But he had merely been further out of sight.

I had truly come home.

Jeff uncorked the bottle, poured, tasted. He gestured with his head and glass for me to take up mine, then lifted his own. He spilled a few drops and said, sharp teeth flashing white in his beard, "This for the future, that for the past, the very gods marvel at what's come to pass."

Together, we drank the blood-dark wine.

MANBAP

"There," said Dr. Krishnamurti.

I obediently looked where he was pointing. The olive drab tidal flat seemed to stretch to infinity. "What?" I asked.

"Right there," he said, leaning closer so I could look down his arm. I smelled his luncheon curry and a faint hint of sweat. The doctor was a traditionalist, at least when it came to diet, and it was hot out in the channeled mud flats. "That darker green patch," he added, "close to the horizon. Your first man-bap."

"Ah," I said, seeing it at last. Without the briefing material I might never have picked that particular shade of blue-green out of the spectrum of dull greens, browns, and grays. I sat back and put a third of a meter or so more distance between the researcher and myself, acutely conscious that I must stink from the hours spent in the landing pod.

"Shall we go closer?"

I dipped my paddle and the red-orange ovoid, a boat hardly big enough for two, slid across the water, rippling the reflection of sky and clouds.

"Ordinarily, this would be for one man," said Krishnamurti, "but without equipment it will do for two." He looked around the horizon. "It is," he added, "highly maneuverable."

"And difficult to sink," I added.

"Precisely."

8334-IV, better known to its inhabitants as Cloud, is five sixths covered by mostly shallow seas. Weather fronts build up rapidly and travel long distances, the reason why Krishnamurti kept scanning the horizon. Out here in the open, our only choice would be to seal ourselves in the hull of our craft and tumble with the waves until the storm passed.

All of the station staff were old hands at this, but I, only a few hours on-world, would have preferred to sleep myself out before my initiation. *Which*, I thought, laying my paddle across my lap and letting Krishnamurti do the final maneuvers, *was exactly what I would have done had I not been swept away by the enthusiastic doctor.*

"You must see the manbap," he had said. "As soon as possible. They are unique, unparalleled on any other world."

So they are, I was tempted to answer, *and they will wait a day, or even two*, but officially Krishnamurti was my immediate superior and there was no need to get off on the wrong foot.

The specimen we stopped near came much closer to being a tree than many things I had seen given the name on other worlds. It was nearly five meters high at two points, and had leathery-looking leaves bigger than my hand.

Neither fact was what first caught one's attention. The plant was in the form of a vast u, supported by a dozen or more knobby legs springing from the bottom curve. Even as we watched the thing tilted inexorably forward, pulling a few spiky roots completely out of the water, and submerging others on the forward side.

"There," said the doctor with satisfaction. "It walks."

It did, after a fashion.

The forward or head section was whichever was the more thriving. As its weight of foliage grew it forced root spikes deeper into the water and the bottom muck. The part of the stem washed by the tides sprouted incipient roots, which began growing in earnest once they were continuously wet. Trailing spikes died off or turned into branches as they were pulled out of the water.

Manbap could hardly be said to gallop across the flats, but they were fast growing, and could move several hundred meters in the course of a year. Enough to escape death when the salinity content of the sea, influenced by tides and storms half a hemisphere away, went beyond their tolerance.

The trees were almost impossible to kill, for any floating piece would send rootlets questing for the bottom, tie itself down and start to grow again. Genetic testing suggested that whole swaths of growth were natural clones.

"Elegant," I told the doctor. "But why, 'manbap?'"

"It is Hindu," he said. "My little joke. 'Manbap' is father-mother. You see the father," he pointed to the taller of the tree's two spires, "followed, as once was quite proper, by the mother." He indicated the trailing arm of the u. "And of course they will have many children."

"Clever," I said.

He looked a little daft, but then most researchers get their specialty on the brain. No problem, I'd met the type before, and would again. I knew from my self-briefing the good doctor was probably saner than most, for he had an outside interest: pre-space-faring Indian history, the British Raj, independence, and the civil insurrections that had resplit the subcontinent between Hindu and Muslim.

"Wonderful," I added.

"Oh, there are many wonders here," he said and grinned as if he had invented, rather than discovered the manbap. "Let us look closer." With three deft strokes, Krishnamurti brought us into the shadow of the tree.

I glanced up nervously.

"It's quite safe," he said.

I took his word for it.

Closer, I could see that the manbap was an ecology unto itself, with yellow false saprophytes clinging to its exposed knees and a school of black-striped pseudo-fish, as long as my finger and with four bulging eyes, hunting darters in the halls and caverns formed by its roots.

Already the mud raised by its "stride" was settling, and leaning over I saw something sinuous as a snake whip across an open space between the new-driven roots. A dozen fronds I had thought plants shrank into themselves, animal-quick, then reopened slowly, seining for disturbed benthic organisms.

The water looked not much more than a meter deep. That

was deceptive, for the layers and layers of rotting matter were so soft that I might sink well over my head before it became firm enough to support me. On-planet laborers were required to wear suits complete with a self-contained air supply.

Krishnamurti and I were making do with skin-tights and soft helms, but when we worked, we too would dress hard. Cloud was a benign world by the usual standards, but that did not make it safe. The more benign, the more likelihood of cross-overs, diseases endemic to the local life but deadly to our alien selves. Not for nothing were we clad in skin-tights with extra filters hanging by their straps, ready to slap across our nose and mouth gear.

Even as I watched a distant manbap released a mist of golden pollen that drifted across the estuary. Krishnamurti slapped his auxiliary filter into place. I followed suit, although as far as I could see the miasma would come nowhere near. We were in greater danger from some tree over the horizon behind us.

The reason for the researcher's caution was apparent a moment later when, one by one, the trees touched by the pollen haze began to release theirs also. Soon there was a fine golden dust over everything, as if the entire world had been gilded. This particular grove was self-triggering.

It was beautiful.

Beautiful death to me and my kind, for the grains germinated in contact with moist tissue, sprouting long, probing pollen tubes that pierced skin and sucked nourishment until the original germ plasm was multiplied a thousand-fold or more and formed a brittle fruiting-body that burst in its turn.

An admirable evolutionary tactician, the manbap, for the simple device stripped biological resources from other life forms at minimal cost to the pollen's genitor. So clever, in fact, that I was here to study it, in the hope that it would be possible to engineer a terraforming plant to do the same.

It is rare to find a world like Cloud where the local life is both well-developed and not-too-hostile to humans. We are finding it pays, in the long view, to take barren balls of stone and build our own man-tailored ecologies. If the rock-eating plants we have devised could convert the energy already gathered by alien life forms, we would be one immense step ahead in producing hospitable environments.

Krishnamurti and I bent to the task of sucking the golden pollen grains into the collection boxes. We knew the priorities. We needed as wide as range of genetic material as possible, and in fairly large quantities, so that the effort to produce terraforming plants could go forward quickly.

Once the appropriate processes were devised, certified, and set in motion, settlers would be sold shares and shipped out on decades-long voyages, sleeping as the worlds they would colonize were terraformed for them. Ships on the shorter passages might have to orbit until their planets were ready, but those that made the long warps would emerge from drive to globes as blue and cloud-girdled as ancient Earth.

Inexpensive terraforming and warp drive capacity have made it possible for each of the larger ethnic groups that once fought so hard on our home world to have a planet of their own. Now only those who care to cooperate need come into space and meet the full spectrum of mankind. In several thousand years some of us will be very different indeed, but that is the future's problem.

For the time being, there is peace among our warring tribes, and those of us who understand the issues at stake are eager to advance the research that can keep it that way. I've gotten more cynical over the decades, but I've never lost my faith in the basic worth of my job as an enabler, tedious though it can be to go the extra distance.

As for manbap pollen, it showed such promise that as soon as the two of us returned from my first expedition our samples were divided and sent up to the ship that had brought me. Despite the cost, it had waited in orbit, ready to carry our harvest to the five principal terraforming laboratories plus half a dozen lottery-winning smaller ones.

As postings went, Cloud was a pleasant one, and after I had learned the safety procedures and survived my first wave-rolling in the tumbling hull of my boat, I went out alone, as did Krishnamurti, so that we might gather the greatest possible variety of specimens.

We generally did not work far apart, it being convenient for both of us to be taken to one location by the station airship and then split the points of the compass between us. As the stronger paddler, Krishnamurti would work against the prevailing wind, while I would work with it. At the end of the day we would rendezvous. The dirigible would come to me, and he would let the wind bring him to us.

Then home, the blue-green of the manbap groves streaming beneath the airship, the endless tide-plain forests broken only by the circular breaks in the canopies that we called lagoons. Krishnamurti and I theorized they were the exhausted sites where the original plants had grown, or perhaps spots where solid bottom was too far down to support the trees.

I had lived in many places, but Cloud was a new experience for me. Although I spent the greater part of my evenings in the lively company of others, I was completely alone when I was out gathering. The frequent storms clotted transmissions with static, so safety signals were simple, strong pulses. There was no on-air chatter here.

I had never been so completely on my own before.

Indeed, station-raised, I had seldom spent much time out of earshot of other people. The floating homes of space-borne mankind are filled with background noise of human beings at work, play, and sleep. So the vast silence of Cloud's mud flats was daunting, at least until my ear grew able to read its language.

There was a shush-shush that meant the tide was retreating, and that my only concern was that I not strand my boat on a mud bar. There was a hiss-plop that meant the water was rising and I should put up the wind-pole and listen for the alarm that meant the satellites saw a storm not far over the horizon.

At first I sang and talked aloud, both from fear of the silence and because the freedom to be noisy was a rare luxury. Then weeks passed and I grew to love the vast, silent groves, and the shy life that hid in them and watched me with alien eyes, the amphibious leaf-hoppers, the slinks, and the pseudo-fish that could see above and below the surface simultaneously.

I seldom penetrated the great swaths of trees. There was no reason to, for the DNA was identical in those plants at the edge and at the heart of the mass. It was as effective, and far easier, to paddle my craft along the seaward side, where the saltier water stunted manbap growth, making the pollen cysts in their crowns more accessible.

The weeks passed, and I became skilled at finding my way through the winding channels between the trees by the sound of the water purling through the spiky roots. There was little else to be heard, for there were no avian forms and Cloud's animal life, tied to the sea, did not vocalize above the surface.

It was a fine, sunny day when merely to be alive, skimming in the dappled shade near the manbap, and feeling the slight burn of muscles working at my personal best, was a joy. Then came the sound that shattered my mood. Not sure what I had heard, I held my stroke, listening. It came again.

A wail punctuated by thrashing, something so odd on this near-silent world that I had to satisfy my curiosity. Already turning my boat, I justified the deviation from routine by telling myself it was for science. The truth was I hoped for unexplored aspect of these plants that would then become attached to my name.

I hungered for a little of the fame that was Krishnamurti's now that the manbap genes were in use wherever terraforming was in progress. The "tree" had an exotic appeal, not just because of its u-shaped trunk and blue-green leaves, but because it "walked." Called the empire plant on seven or eight worlds, its recombined genes had conquered near-barren rock for us.

Heart beating fast, I paddled into the dusky light of the grove, climbing onto the buttressed roots to lift my craft over tangles that impeded the channel. My suit slimed to the knees with rot that I could smell through two filters, I began to regret my impulsiveness. It was an eerie place.

All around me, clustered on the knees and spires of the manbap, were masses of white false saprophyte. Although its yellow and orange cousins are found well down into the salt zone, ghost fingers grows only where the water is as near drinkable as it ever is, unfiltered, on Cloud.

Kilometers from any shore yet I wondered if there might be an underground spring here—a flaw between layers of rock that let fresh water leak into the ocean. If so, I must map it and drop a beacon, for on sea-swept Cloud a reliable source of potable water is as precious as oil is on some worlds.

I had nearly decided to go back, when I saw sunshine ahead. In a few more easy strokes I paddled out into a lagoon. The surface was still and clear, reflecting the deep azure sky. Looking around me, I regretted the necessity of reporting fresh water, if it were there. Only when I looked into the shadow of the trees did I see the bone yard on the bottom.

There were skeletons in every stage of disarticulation, although all, with one exception, had been stripped of flesh. Phalanxes from flippers littered the bottom and the curving arcs of spinal rods and brace ribs lay heaped or scattered as the tide and the currents had left them.

The one exception was a pseudo-fish, the kind we on Cloud call a grouper, for although it had four eyes, stubby fins and a tail set horizontally rather than vertically, that was what it most resembled. Large as my torso, it struggled, pierced through with roots that grew even as I watched. It was this creature's high-pitched moans and thrashing that I had heard.

Despite the danger I paddled one stroke forward, drawn by

the gaze of one enormous eye. I had been fishing on my home world, had caught and eaten my share of trout, but there was something piteous and aware in this creature's look, as if it could see me and hoped for help.

Even as I watched it twitched and died.

My relief at the end of the grouper's pain was tempered by the thought that it was a long way back and the manbap might find my alien flesh nearly as attractive as that of the native life form. I turned my boat with another stroke, only to find that the way had closed behind me.

It was probably the worst moment of my life.

I am not brave. Life on a research ship does not require bravery, and those reckless enough to attempt to practice it usually die young. In space your instincts play you false. Emergencies must be met with a cool head and well-trained re-sponses. Trapped in a situation I did not know how to deal with I did the logical thing.

I panicked.

The manbap had shifted toward the fresh corpse, exploring the nourishment with questing tendrils. This had left the far side of the tree ring thinner and less obstructed. It was my good fortune that it was toward this weaker section that I drove my boat with terror-enhanced strength.

Trusting to my suit to protect my flesh, I swung my paddle. As I chopped and hacked, I could hear fibers rasp across the hardened surface that shielded my back. I swatted tendrils from before my face and would, at that moment, have given almost anything to be dealing with the familiar fear of riding out a storm on the bottom.

I could not seal up. It might take days for the airship to find me if I cocooned, for in the grove my recall signal might be echoed and re-echoed by the wood of the feeding trees until it was too faint to detect. Base might assume that I was dead, for an accident that would destroy my boat's hull and its embedded transponder would certainly have destroyed me.

I was on my own. With the high hum of my recycler as background noise to my attempt to fight free, I wondered how long I could sustain so violent a level of activity. Once the unit shut down, I would go comatose from lack of oxygen until enough penetrated my filters. It was poor consolation to know that I might not feel it when the carnivorous manbap began to feed.

Carbon dioxide alarm shrilling, I burst out into the surge of the channel. I leaned forward, panting, listening to the clicks and hums of my life support unit as it strove to make up my deficit, and tried not to think of the fish, writhing in mortal agony as an alien watched and did nothing.

Presently the alarm shut off and I recovered enough to look around me. To my relief, there was every sign of a coming storm. There would be no awkward questions if I set off a beacon and asked to be retrieved early. It was standard operating procedure.

I wanted to think about what I had seen before I brought the matter to official attention. I was convinced that Krishnamurti, so intensely interested and with so much experience, knew of the peril hidden within the groves and had not told me or anyone else. The question was, why? There had been something that first day, something in that bold yet evasive eye—

I had barely punched the tab on my recall before the station flipped up the flag that told me the airship was already on its way. Evidently they had noticed the approaching bad weather before I had. In minutes, one dirigible crewman picked me out of the waves while another signaled Krishnamurti that he was next. There was no confirmation.

"Odd," said Chayama, "he's usually one of the first to call in."

"Even when it isn't needed," said Blauberg, the pilot, eyes on the ragged horizon line.

We moved slowly into the wind, signaling as we went, scanning the waves for Krishnamurti's boat. When we had gone beyond the farthest possible limit, Blauberg cut the power to the engines and let us drift back, signaling over the area we had already covered. Still nothing but the rising sea and the blue-gray of manbap leaves lashed by the wind.

"Maybe he's hurt," I said reluctantly. I had been out most of the day and my terrorized flight had drained me. Not eager to go back into the water, I did not want to explain why. I had a few bones to pick with the wily doctor. Enablers learn to be discreet.

"Gone to the bottom early," suggested Gonzales.

"Um," grunted the pilot. "If we're going to put a man in, it'll have to be soon."

There was something at the edge of a dense grove, something red-orange, pinned against the buttressed roots of the trees. As I watched, it rolled free and wallowed in the froth-streaked waves, then went under. If it were the boat, its trim was entirely wrong, as if the ballast tanks had not been filled, but the hull had flooded.

"There's no point to putting a man down unless we have a fix on Krishnamurti's position," said the co-pilot. I felt the hard knot in my stomach loosen. Blauberg was in no hurry. I knew the drill. They would not urge me to take to the water unreasonably.

I had been the only one to see the researcher's swamped craft. The pilot was busy at his instruments and the two crewmen had taken the bow and other side of the craft to scan. I was, for an instant, tempted to say nothing. Then the red-orange form tumbled into view again.

"There," I yelled and pointed.

It was obviously the boat, rolling over and over, unsealed.

"Got away from him?" said Chayama.

Blauberg swung the ocular around and we all took a close look.

The craft was scuffed and banged about, but basically undamaged. Krishnamurti could have survived in it. We snagged it and winched it up: equipment is expensive and if the researcher proved difficult to find, it might have a clue.

"So where is he?" the pilot asked himself, and set the ocular controls for a search pattern. Slaved to the device the airship's engines hummed and groaned as it maintained position. Human vision is sometimes more discriminating than machine. The crewmen and I scanned the tumble of wind-whipped leaves and froth-topped waves, hoping for a glimpse of Krishnamurti's yellow suit.

Despite my suspicion the researcher had concealed vital information, I don't think I was less than thorough. It was mere coincidence that it was Gonzales who picked him out first, half-submerged by the stout trunk that he had sheltered against. "There," the crewman said, not loud, and the rest of us knew he thought the man dead.

I put the short-distance earpiece in and closed the fastenings on my own red suit, then looped my arms into the fittings on the safety cable and stepped to the hatch as Chayama swung it wide. I'm sure I looked willing enough, but in my heart I would have given a year's pay not to be the one on the line.

I stepped out into space and swung vertiginously until I landed, up to my knees in water, amid battering leaves and branches. The vegetation was so thick that I had to have the crewman direct me even though I was not six meters from place where Krishnamurti's suit had been sighted.

"Right in front of you," Gonzales yelled in my ear. I forced foliage-heavy twigs aside, shuddering at the sound of wood raking over my protective shell, made my legs move by sheer willpower. I felt like I'd left my stomach on the airship droning and humming above me.

I don't know. I'd seen the fish, you see, or I might have believed it was an accident, that scavengers had already been at the corpse. But when I saw the skull lolling within the helmet, the fibers driven into the double filters, I knew that the manbap had gotten Krishnamurti.

"He's dead," I said to the hovering observers.

"You're sure," said the pilot.

"Yes," I said, feeling the safety cable pull at me, the suck of fast-rising water at my waist. The storm was very close. There was a shift in the pitch of the engine noise. "There's nothing but bones in the suit."

"We've lost the right engine," said Chayama in my ear.

"Abandon him in place," said the pilot. For a terrified moment I thought he meant me. Then, "Ready?" he asked me. I wasn't going to say no—I checked my lashings.

"Reeling in," said Gonzales to someone else, and I saw the world slew slantwise as the wind took me. The horizon line bisected my vision, there was a tug at my ankles, and someone slammed the hatch. After the howl of the wind and the clawing branches, the silence in the cabin seemed wonderful.

"From the sea we came, to the sea we return," muttered Blauberg, hands maneuvering us up and around so we could scud away from the lighting-stabbed clouds.

"Ashes to ashes," murmured the crewmen and I. "Dust to dust."

Uncomfortable in the suit I would not shuck until we reached base, I sat back. There would be a lot of explaining to do, and then a lot of recriminations. I could only hope that Krishnamurti's notes were much more complete than his orientation tours. There were manbap genes scattered over the choicest of the new worlds.

ONE SUMMER EVENING

Summer was the cruelest season. As the decades passed, the often-thwarted hope that he might heal had faded into despair, almost indifference, but when the long golden days came they always reminded him of what he once was and renewed his pain.

He knit his long fingers together and sighed. The girl laughed at him whenever she caught him in this mood, and he had become skilled at concealing his disquietude from her, if not from the three cats that lounged before the fire kept burning day and night regardless of the weather. Wiser than any human, they fled to the jungle safety of the garden whenever he unclasped the dark book bound in scaly leather.

So far the girl, chosen for her sunny personality—for he had a horror of clever women—had been right not to take him seriously. The book was as useless as he himself and might have gone to start the kitchen fire on some winter morning, except of course that the stove used gas.

Left knee creaking, he got to his feet to pace. That he had been exhausted when he had placed himself here at the conclusion of his failed labors was no excuse. What had then seemed overwhelmingly desirable, an obscure life filled with simple routines and mundane pleasures, was now not even tolerable. *Grief is always a bad counselor*, he reminded himself.

The hoarse, mechanical wail of a distant siren marred the summer air, and he frowned. When he had bound himself, he had known it would take great expertise to reverse the process. A delicate balance of influences had to be reached before he, with the, metaphorically speaking, small lever that was all he had allowed himself to retain, could once again move worlds.

Not being a total fool, even when grieving, he had not meant to make it impossible to change his mind. He was, after all, human, or nearly so. Still, in the end, his craft had failed him, or perhaps, in the prime of his powers he had underestimated what the loss of them would mean to him.

Turning, he looked out the open French doors. A late-evening mist was forming over the river. The garden's trunks, twigs, and leaves were picked and edged with poignant rose sunset. The sounds of the works of modern men grew dull and distant. Yet another perfect moment for the testing spell. He smiled bitterly. There had been many such.

And nothing had happened. How often he had sat waiting, offended by the distant rumble of airplanes, until the cats returned home and the girl came in from the kitchen. Redolent of herbs, spices, plus her own warm musk, she would lean on the arm of his chair and charm him into a better mood with wiles older than any man's.

Still, he thought, *I will not let this opportunity pass. If nothing else, I would always wonder if this was the time.* Taking the book from the shelf, he sat down, unclasped it, and smoothed the page carefully. Yet another try before he turned the television on for the evening and poured the first of what would be one too many drinks, if the girl did not beguile him to some other occupation. Checkers, chess, or the eroticisms that revealed a little too plainly how long it had been since she was as naive as she liked to pretend.

I cannot grudge her little deceit, he thought. *How long has it been since I was an innocent? Never, perhaps, given my parentage and childhood. She does well by me, and old men must make compromises young ones would never admit. Glory is the stuff of youth, as diplomacy is of age.*

Focusing his mind, he reread the instructions he had penned so long ago. He trusted that older self as he did not trust his present one. Besides, magicking from memory without dire need was ostentatious. He had always preferred discretion when discretion would serve as well or better than showy workings.

Somewhere beyond the garden wall a car hooted urgently and was answered by an angry chorus of horns. He winced, then spread his hands and spoke, feeling his tongue twist and curl reluctantly around syllables never meant for any human mouth. As he spoke, the hide on the book shuddered against his thighs, as if it were a living thing, stirring in deep sleep.

Or perhaps his legs had quivered with the obscure tensions of age. The signs were on him. He had not much longer, and he had never believed in anything other than the four powers, earth, air, fire, and water. They had served him, and he, they. Having gone beyond the appearance to the reality, he tried to be—

Begin, said a voice in his mind and he did. Spell muttered and sighed into the summer twilight, he leaned back, eyes closed. The scrabble of a cat's claws on the hearth bricks woke him from his doze. The gray tabby had caught a mouse or, the ancient exile leaned forward in his chair, perhaps it was a bat.

Eyes narrowing suddenly, he held out a hand and compelled the animal to him with a skill long disused. Then he prodded the small carcass with a long forefinger before giving it back to its rightful owner.

Head high to keep the wings from dragging, the offended tabby carried the tiny dragon off to its private lair under the blackberry brambles. The other two cats drew as near as they dared, and crouched, tails lashing, hissing. In the silence, you could hear the plop and ripple of the river.

Hands palm up, open, on the book in his lap, he felt power begin to fill the hollow in his soul. A swirl of vapor formed above the garden's beech trees. Looking up from its fabulous feast, the gray tabby yowled. Fat raindrops splattered the paving, wept down the glass of the open French doors. Black, white, and gray, the cats bolted into the house as the first stroke of lightening slashed the air. Thunder walked the sky.

Merlin laughed.

www.ingramcontent.com/pod-product-compliance
Lightning Source LLC
Chambersburg PA
CBHW020152180626
46810CB00004B/1860

* 9 7 8 0 9 8 3 9 5 8 8 9 3 2 *